The Admiral's Lady

MARY ANN GIBBS

The Admiral's Lady

 MASON /CHARTER

NEW YORK 1975

© Mary Ann Gibbs 1974

First published in the U.S. by Mason/Charter
Publishers, Inc., 384 Fifth Ave., N.Y.C.

First printing, March 1975
Second printing, June 1975

Library of Congress Cataloging in Publication Data

Gibbs, Mary Ann.
  The Admiral's lady.

  First published in 1974 under title: A wife for the Admiral.
  I. Title.
PZ4.G44Ad3 [PR6057.1234]   823'.9'14   74–23049
ISBN 0–88405–099–8

1

Susanna Farebrother looked disconsolately out of the drawing-room windows at the rain, and then she turned to her aunt in the room behind her, busy stitching at a tennis blouse for her niece—a most workmanlike garment in blue and white stripes, to be worn with a blue skirt. 'Why,' she asked, 'does it elect to rain just when you most particularly need it to be fine?'

'In May,' Dinah Woodcock replied serenely, 'the weather is as unpredictable as it is in April. Warm sunshine—such as we had last week—is often followed by thunder, hailstorms and even snow.'

'Snow! What a home-coming that would be for Papa!' Susanna laughed and then sobered quickly, as much a thing of moods as the weather. 'Two and a half years since he was here, and now that he is coming home for good it is raining! I wish he had not gone to see Uncle Will in Paris. It was so beautiful last week when he could have come home, and a rainy day would have suited Uncle Will as well as any other, I'm sure!' She paused, but her aunt was silent, her head bent over the blouse. 'Aunt Dinah, how well did you know Uncle Will?'

'I only met him once at your father's wedding,' Dinah said non-committally.

'And did you like him?'

'Not very much.' She did not add that her opinion of him had been influenced by her sister Mary, Susanna's mother, who had detested her brother-in-law and had

5

not troubled to hide it. 'One cannot judge a man on such short acquaintance.'

'I could,' said Susanna decidedly. At eighteen she was a very decided person, with strong likes and dislikes. 'Was he very like Papa in those days?'

'Oh yes. They are identical twins. I teased your mother on her wedding-day by telling her it was lucky John was in uniform or she might easily have married the wrong man.'

'I remember him years ago coming to stay here at Waveney while we were at the Grange. Grandmamma had just died and he came to see Papa after the funeral and I liked him. He had a gentle way with him and a soft way of talking. Not like Papa and his quarter-deck voice!' She imitated the absent Admiral Sir John Farebrother. ' "It's an *order*!" ' I remember thinking that I must find a way of knowing them apart. Everyone teased me because they were so very much alike.' Those two handsome men, looking down at the puzzled seven-year-old, both blue-eyed and fair-haired, with thin faces and the same voices and laughter. And yet not quite the same laughter, if you happened to be gazing up at them as she had done. Her Uncle Will wrinkled his nose when he laughed, whereas Papa's nose came down in a beak. That was the difference she had discovered between them and she kept it to herself in case, if she told them of her discovery, her uncle would pull down his nose and her papa would wrinkle his just to confuse her. They played such pranks on people when they were schoolboys, she had been told. In fact there had been three whole weeks when Will had gone to stay with some people in Scotland where John had been invited, and they never found out that all the time John had been in the Isle of Wight, learning to sail a boat.

'I wish I'd been born a twin,' she sighed, and then with another swift change of mood, 'Shall I have a bustle, do you think? For my first ball-dress I mean? Ella Somerton's had a cage in hers. It made her look like a horse in a pantomime. I do think bustles are ugly. I wish we could go back to crinolines. I can just remember Mamma's crinoline when she came to say good night to me in the nursery before going out with Papa to a ball. She looked so lovely.'

'Mrs. Somerton had Ella's dress made by Madame Smythe,' Dinah said thoughtfully. 'She suggested that I should buy yours at Debenham and Freebody's, but I do not like ready-made dresses.'

'Neither do I like Madame Smythe. Why doesn't she call herself Mrs. Smith—affected little woman? And she is so refined that she makes me nervous.' She twisted up her mouth, mimicking the good lady. ' "Just a leetle bit shorter I think, Miss Farebrother—a fraction of an inch above the ankles—as you are not yet out." My coming-out ball-dress will sweep the floor *and* it will have a train. But I am not so certain about a bustle.'

'You are tall and slender enough to wear one.' Dinah examined her niece's figure critically. 'Ella was too short and podgy.' They fell comfortably silent and the Admiral's old retriever, Bruce, got up from the hearthrug and waddled over to his young mistress, putting his nose into her hand.

'Darling Bruce! Your master will be here very soon. But don't go mad with excitement, my love, or you will have a heart attack and that would be a dreadful homecoming for Papa. Aunt Dinah, now that Papa is coming home for good, do you think he will marry again?'

'Will what, child?'

'Marry again. Papa. Aunt Dinah, you are not listening to me!'

'I beg your pardon, Susanna. My thoughts were far away.' Far away down the years at her sister's wedding, with the twin brothers, John and Will, waiting at the

7

altar rails for Mary. Poor Mary had never had a good word for her husband's twin, calling him dissolute, foot-loose and fancy-free. He was lazy, she said, and good for nothing except playing at being an artist. Mary, who had married John Farebrother because he would inherit Waveney and a baronetcy and who never lived to be 'my lady'.

Susanna was ten when her mother died and her aunt, Mary's younger sister, had come to take charge of the Grange and John's little daughter while he was away at sea. And when two years later his father died and they had moved to the Manor House, Dinah had reluctantly taken on the larger responsibility that it entailed, feeling her way with the old servants who were inclined to resent her giving orders in their master's absence. What could the younger daughter of an impoverished country squarson know about the running of a place like Waveney?

'I wish Papa could marry you,' Susanna said thoughtfully. 'It would be so nice to have you as my step-mamma. I don't know anybody I'd like so much.' Then after a moment she added, 'I would not object to Dorothea, of course. She is the only one I would tolerate in your place, Aunt Dinah.'

Dinah did not answer for a moment and then she said quietly, 'A man may not marry his dead wife's sister, my dear.'

'I know, and I think it is a very stupid law, and if I were in Parliament I should alter it very quickly.'

'As there is little prospect of you ever being in Parliament, except in the Ladies' Gallery, I do not think you will be able to alter it, though.'

Susanna moved restlessly to the fireplace, Bruce following her, and as she went down on her knees beside her aunt he resumed his old position on the rug. 'I do want Papa to be in a good temper when he comes home,' she said, her hand caressing the old dog's head. 'Aunt Dinah, do you think he will approve of Frank?'

'If you are referring to Captain Sloane I have no doubt he will approve of him as he would of any other young man of good family,' Dinah said steadily. 'But as he is only a captain in a line regiment and has no money beyond his pay—which is not enough to keep him without assistance from his father—I do not think your papa will encourage any closer tie, my love.'

'Oh, Aunt Di!' Susanna moved impatiently. She was a very pretty girl, with her mother's lovely hazel eyes, black-lashed, and quite a bit of her father's temper. Mrs. Somerton, the Bishop's wife, said perhaps with some truth that Susanna Farebrother was spoilt. 'You are being very cruel!'

'My darling, you are only eighteen.'

'What of it? My mother was married at eighteen. And I shall be nineteen next month at my coming-out ball.'

'And ever since you were sixteen you have been falling in love with somebody—once, not so very long ago, with a man old enough to be your father!'

Susanna had the grace to blush. 'But you must admit that he was very fascinating, Aunt Di!'

'Fascinating!' Her aunt sniffed. 'He was much too stout, too fond of his food, he had greasy black hair—and he was a foreigner,' she concluded, as if that clinched the matter.

Susanna laughed, 'I could never have married him, anyway. There were at least three impediments in the way, his wife and two children in Italy!' She sighed and went back to the window to watch the rain. 'I am so madly in love with Frank!'

'But you were only introduced to him at Christmas, child.'

'I know, but I have seen him about in Jerningham the

whole winter while he has been staying with Miss Dudley for the hunting season, and he is so handsome that I couldn't help falling in love with him at first sight. And directly he spoke to me I knew that he was the only man I could ever love.'

'What is more important, my dear—is he in love with you?' From her own observation of the young man in question Dinah Woodcock had put him down as a good-looking flirt, on the look-out for a rich wife, but she was ready to allow that she might be prejudiced, being a middle-aged spinster of thirty-six.

'I am almost sure he is,' Susanna said softly. Had he not stolen a kiss last night, when they were in the Bishop's conservatory, on the occasion of Mrs. Somerton's musical evening for young people in which, as her coming-out ball was such a little way away, she had been included as well as Ella's younger sister Maud?

From the day of Mrs. Taverner's Christmas party, however, Captain Sloane had singled her out from other girls. She remembered that evening as if it were yesterday: they had started by playing Charades, following it by Stage Coach and then Forfeits and after that Dutch Concert, and as the fun grew more uproarious, the Captain managed to monopolise Miss Farebrother, asking her why he had never met her before.

'Because I'm not out yet,' she replied, aware that his eyes were telling her that she was the prettiest girl in the room. 'My coming-out ball is to be on the fourteenth of June.'

'I cannot wait for it to come,' he said, and then Ella had called to them jealously to play Pope Joan.

But last night during the musical evening they had gone into the conservatory at the Palace to get cool, as the drawing-room was very warm, and in admiring some of the ferns there Susanna had got her hair caught in an overhanging palm. Captain Sloane had left Ella to go back to the drawing-room alone while he hurried back to help, and as he did so, there being nobody else but themselves there at that time, he kissed her. 'Forgive me,' he whispered. 'But you are quite adorable.'

Susanna had gone home with her head in a whirl. A man, she argued, would not kiss a girl unless he was in love with her. Or would he? Her knowledge of men was but slight, culled from novels in which the heroes were handsome and manly and noble—and the villains black as ink.

That was last night, the culmination of many meetings at the Palace, where he had got into the habit of neglecting the plain and grown-up Ella for her pretty friend, and at the houses of Mrs. Taverner and the Honourable Iris Dudley, both ladies having their own reasons for entertaining the Admiral's daughter.

'There's only one thing for it,' Susanna said now, 'Papa will have to get married again, and as he cannot marry you it will have to be Dorothea. And then he will be so sweet-tempered that he will be pleased to have me married too.' She broke off. 'Somebody's riding up to the house—who can it be on a day like this? I believe— yes, it is!—that detestable Mr. Royde. I hope he is not going to call on us when we expect Papa at any minute.'

'I don't know why you dislike Mr. Royde so much,' said her aunt mildly.

'For the very reason that I find him dislikable.' Susanna tossed her head. 'He treats me like a child.'

'Perhaps because you behave like one.'

'I do not!' Susanna watched with dismay as the rider approached the front of the house and after attaching his mount to the rail at the foot of the steps, mounted them with some determination. 'He's coming in!' she said with disgust.

But Mr. Royde did not come in. They heard his voice speaking to Perryman the butler as he opened the door

11

and there the matter would have ended, had not Bruce heard his voice too. Now Bruce happened to love Mr. Royde as much as Susanna detested him, and he got to his feet, taking no notice of his young mistress's peremptory call to him to come back, and having thrust open the door with his nose, dashed into the hall to greet their visitor with wagging tail, short barks of welcome and a great show of affection.

Susanna hurried after him and tried to drag him away. 'I beg your pardon, Mr. Royde,' she said breathlessly, scarlet with vexation, 'but Bruce is expecting Papa—as we all are at any moment.'

'So your butler told me.' Mr. Royde's eyes rested on her with a gleam of sardonic amusement. 'And as I have no wish to intrude on you just now—and am in any case too wet for a lady's drawing-room—I will be on my way.'

'You *are* much too wet for a drawing-room, aren't you?' Susanna agreed, looking at him resentfully and disliking the cool tone in which he had spoken, and Dinah came out into the hall in time to hear her.

'Mr. Royde,' she said, holding out her hand to him with a reproving look at her niece. 'Do come in. Perryman will take your wet things and I daresay he can find you a pair of the Admiral's slippers.'

'I would not dream of troubling him. My mission was not important, merely a letter for the Admiral about the new village school which is to be built, half on my land and half on his. Will you please tell him that I have had the plans from the architect and they are ready for his approval directly he has the time to look at them? It was too wet to bring them with me today. Goodbye, Miss Woodcock. Goodbye, Miss Farebrother.' And he was gone.

'Susanna, how can you be so rude to a neighbour?' Miss Woodcock spoke with real distress as they went back to the drawing-room together, but Susanna was not in the least ashamed.

'I detest him and he knows it,' she said. 'I am glad he had the sense to go when he did.' She gave no quarter where Mr. Royde was concerned and she expected none. She had learned from Ella that he seldom went to balls and never danced when he did. She had every reason to hope that he would not come to her coming-out ball, and that if he did he would only grace the card-room with his presence.

Ella Somerton was annoyed that he did not dance. In her eyes he was quite the most eligible bachelor in the neighbourhood, being extremely rich, and with a large estate that joined Waveney. But Mr. Royde showed no inclination to change his state; his widowed sister, Lady Sare, lived with him and he seemed to be perfectly satisfied with the arrangement. He was a good-looking man of thirty, with an austere manner that did not make him popular in Jerningham, their county town, boasting a cathedral and a close. He was too much occupied with his estate and its tenants, it was said, and he took an absurdly keen interest in the draining of his land and the upkeep of his hedges and his fine stone walls and in keeping his ditches clear. It was said to be the best-kept estate in the county, but while his sister, Lady Sare, was loved by everybody, her brother was not a social success.

Susanna had not quite decided if Edward Royde were a villain, entirely black, but she suspected it. 'He has such a sarcastic way of speaking to you, and a horrid way of looking down his aristocratic nose at you—as if you were a beetle.'

'But he can be very charming, Susie. I expect you are too young for him.'

'A gentleman should show some interest in a person, however young they are,' Susanna said resentfully. Then

13

she forgot about the irritating Mr. Royde and cried excitedly, 'Aunt Dinah, I can see the carriage! It is turning in at the gates. Quickly, come into the hall to welcome him! Bruce, old fellow, get up and come along too—your master is home!'

The Waveney carriage was indeed making its way in at the gates and continued across the park, the coachman, Honeysett, and the groom bending their heads against the driving rain, their tall hats and waterproof capes shining with water. As it approached, Susanna could not wait any longer: she ran out into the hall with Bruce bustling behind her, uttering barks of joy at the name of 'master', which meant only one person in his world. She called to Perryman to come quickly and open the door: he was there much too slowly for her liking and she was struggling with the heavy latch when he caught up with her.

'Now then, you take and let me do that, Miss Susanna', he said. 'The H'Admiral won't be across the park yet, nor anything like.' Behind him the housekeeper, Mrs. Beswick, had hurried out to greet the Admiral on his home-coming and stood waiting at the foot of the stairs.

The door was open at last and through the rain they saw the carriage rapidly approaching and the Admiral himself at the window, waving to them all.

2

The idea that the Admiral should marry again had been started some time ago by the Bishop's wife, Mrs. Somerton. Ever since they had moved to the Manor, Susanna had shared the Somertons' governess, being driven in to the Palace every day by Honeysett, and fetched home at night. Her own governess, Miss Trot, was not capable of teaching the subjects that the Bishop's wife thought essential for the education of her girls, and Dinah, knowing how hard-pressed the Admiral—then only a Vice-Admiral—was for money, had been at her wit's end to know what to do for her niece.

'I'm afraid Dinah Woodcock is a poor tool where Susanna's upbringing is concerned,' Mrs. Somerton told her husband when the offer for Susanna to share their governess had been made and gratefully accepted. 'The child ought to have a governess like our Miss Bentley all the time, of course, but no, Miss Woodcock still keeps on with poor old Trot, who is really only fit to keep the child practising her scales and that sort of thing. Miss Woodcock should know better than that: the Woodcocks are a good family, if they do not have any money.' Here she was wrong, because Dinah knew as well as the Bishop's wife that Susanna needed a clever governess to teach her, just as she was fully aware of the short-comings of poor old Miss Trot, but she had the advantage of being cheap, and if they turned her out she would have nowhere else to go. And having known poverty in her old home where there had been

15

nothing but a constant and despairing effort to keep up appearances, Dinah's heart ruled her common sense.

In spite of her criticism, which was extended to all her friends and acquaintances, the Bishop's wife had a warm affection for Dinah, recognising her good qualities and her devotion to the Admiral and his daughter, and it was just before Sir John Farebrother came home on his previous leave, two and a half years ago, that she had begun talking of the advantages a stepmamma could bring to Susanna.

'You see, my dear,' she told Dinah with her usual forthrightness, 'we know that she is not sixteen yet and at the moment you are all that she needs as chaperon and companion. She is very fond of you, Miss Woodcock. But she will not stay at this age for ever, and she shows promise of being quite a pretty girl when she is older.' Mrs. Somerton would never indulge in warm praise for girls other than her own daughters. 'It would be wiser for her to have a married lady as her chaperon once she starts going to balls, and although she is welcome to come with my girls under my wing, as you know, I do consider that the Admiral will need a mistress for his house once he is home for good.'

And while Dinah was silent, secretly resenting this interference on the part of the Bishop's wife, the good lady added fuel to the fire by saying that directly the Admiral came home on leave she would give some dinner-parties for him.

'There are several ladies I can think of right away who would like to meet him. Miss Dudley, for instance, would make him a charming wife. A thoroughly nice woman, and so well connected, and accustomed to London Society. She would soon correct any little coltish ways that dear Susanna has developed with great tact and understanding. I always think too when a man's wife has a title of her own—if it is only an

Honourable—it does lend a certain *éclat* to the union.'

And while Dinah tried to digest the Honourable Iris Dudley without showing annoyance because her beloved Susanna was accused of having coltish ways that her aunt was apparently not qualified to correct, Mrs. Somerton continued:

'And then there is Mrs. Taverner—our newcomer to the Close! Perhaps not so well bred as dear Miss Dudley—the widow of a City magnate my dear!—but so *rich*!'

Sometimes, Dinah thought, the Bishop's wife had an almost vulgar appreciation of money, and though she did not think Mrs. Somerton could be aware that John Farebrother had come into a bankrupt property when his father died, she evidently considered that he ought to be grateful to anybody who had the kindness to put a fortune in his way. But Dinah very much doubted if he would be grateful: he had a liking for managing his private affairs in his own way.

When the first of the promised dinner-parties was given for him at the Palace on that last leave of his she had watched him anxiously, sitting nearly opposite him in her shabby black evening gown. She saw that he listened to Mrs. Taverner's sprightly conversation with a slightly amused air, and that after dinner he had praised Miss Dudley's pianoforte solo with just the right amount of warmth, but when she had asked his opinion of the ladies afterwards he had said that Mrs. Taverner had seemed a pleasant sort of woman, 'but a deal too rich for me, my dear!' and that he thought Miss Dudley could have put more feeling into her playing. And the twinkle in his eye as he said good night showed her that he knew exactly what the Bishop's wife had been after.

But although Mrs. Somerton had not been successful in her quest for a wife for the Admiral, it had made

17

Dinah think that she was right, and that a married lady would be a much better chaperon for her beloved Susie than a maiden aunt. And because she was accustomed to talking things over with Susanna she had discussed it with her, and they both found that Dorothea Ashworth was by far their favourite runner in the Admiral's stakes.

When John Farebrother had discovered the crippled condition of his inheritance, he had to decide whether he should continue at the Grange and let the Manor, or to move into the Manor—which had been his home until he married—and let the Grange. The latter alternative appealed to him most, and he was fortunate in finding a retired naval officer, Captain Ashworth, to become his tenant.

Captain Ashworth had served with him on the same ship when they were midshipmen, and his family now consisted of a married son in London and an unmarried daughter, Dorothea, living with him, his wife being dead.

The Captain played chess and the Admiral enjoyed a game. They were happy to renew their old friendship while Dorothea became equally friendly with Dinah and Susanna. The families met frequently and continued to meet during the Admiral's absences at sea, and although Dorothea was not even an Honourable, Dinah and her niece considered she would make the ideal stepmamma for Susanna and the perfect wife for the Admiral in years to come.

Certainly he had encouraged her to write to him during this last voyage of his to the China Station, but probably that may have been because Captain Ashworth admitted he was too lazy to write letters, and in any case those that Dorothea wrote for her father were missives that anybody could have read with impunity. They consisted entirely of village news, of her father's

18

gout and the words he had had with their neighbour, Major Worplesdon at Worplesdon Lodge, over certain cucumbers that had been better grown by the Captain's jobbing gardener at the Grange than by the Major's head man at the Lodge. They had light-heartedly touched on scandals that lasted nine days and were forgotten, they gave him news of Susanna, and they were in fact very satisfactory letters for a man to receive when he put into port after weeks at sea. But as he never mentioned them except in his letters to the Captain, both Dinah and Susanna had to own that their effect on him could not be very deep.

But now the Admiral had given up his career at sea for the far more satisfactory one of a country gentleman on his estate at Waveney, and as she caught sight of his face at the carriage window Susanna waved frantically and would have run down the steps into the rain had not her aunt held her back.

'Susie, control yourself, dear!' Was this what Mrs. Somerton had meant by coltish behaviour? 'You will get soaked and your father will not be here any sooner. You had much better wait for him here in the dry.'

Impatiently Susanna waited and the carriage stopped in the drive at last, the groom was down from the box and had the door open and Sir John was out and coming up the steps. Susanna ran down to meet him and flung her arms round his neck.

'Welcome home, Papa!' she cried. 'Welcome home!'

'You'll knock me down, child, if you are so boisterous!' He kept his arm round her and stooped to kiss her and then went up the steps with her into the hall.

'Welcome home, John!' Dinah said. He turned to her quickly with a faint air of embarrassment and took the hand she held out to him and then let it drop.

'Thank you, Dinah,' he said, and almost with an air

19

of relief went on to shake Perryman by the hand and to greet Mrs. Beswick. 'I'm looking forward to those preserves of yours, Mrs. Bess!' he said.

'It was Mr. Will who liked them best, Sir John,' she reminded him sadly. 'How was Mr. Will when you saw him in Paris, sir? I wish he would come to Waveney sometimes.'

'He was working hard, Mrs. Bess. Working hard.' Again there came the faint air of embarrassment. 'Jobson is dealing with the luggage,' he told Perryman. 'He would not trust any of it to the porters at Jerningham.' The Admiral's valet had met him at Southampton and accompanied him to Paris on his way home.

'I don't blame him, sir,' Perryman said darkly. 'Them porters—if they can label a package wrong and send it flying off to Scotland or to Timbuctoo they will.'

The Admiral smiled and followed Dinah and Susanna into the drawing-room, Susanna scolding the old dog Bruce because after a sniff at the Admiral's legs and a faint wag of his tail he had retired at once and stretched himself out on the hearthrug again.

'He must be getting forgetful in his old age,' Susanna said. 'He has never done this before when you come home, Papa. I was afraid he might have a heart attack with his transports of delight. Bruce! Don't you know your master?'

The magic word roused the dog again. He lifted his head, looked round the room, and then ignoring the Admiral settled down again by the hearth.

'He *has* forgotten you!' Susanna said, grieved. 'Oh, poor old Bruce. To think that he could forget the one person he loved best in all the world.'

'Much must be forgiven him, because he is old,' Dinah said. She regarded the Admiral thoughtfully: his small imperial beard was greyer than it used to be, she thought

—it was possible now to distinguish the grey hairs among the fair ones on his chin. She had been a little bit hurt by the coolness of his greeting and remembered Mrs. Somerton's words, that he needed a wife, and a new interest at Waveney.

He had always said how much he looked forward to retirement, but now that it had come he might be regretting the life he had left behind. After all, he had been at sea since he was sixteen.

Tea was set out in the morning-room, and as he tackled a slice of his favourite plum cake Susanna questioned him about the drive from Jerningham station. 'I told Honeysett to be sure to bring you round by the new park,' she said. 'I hope he did?'

'He did indeed, much to my annoyance. Why he wanted to go so far out of the way on a day like this when I only wanted to get home I cannot imagine.'

Dinah looked at him, puzzled. 'I suppose he thought you would like to see how far they had got with it,' she said.

'Is the board with the name of it up inside the gates?' asked Susanna eagerly. 'It is to be a black board with gold lettering. And what did you think of the gates? Aunt Dinah and I chose them from an illustrated book of ironwork.'

'Did you indeed?' He looked surprised.

'The Mayor brought the book himself and we spent nearly a whole morning looking at them,' she told him.

'Well, in that case you should feel very honoured,' said her papa, 'to be asked to select the pattern for some new park gates by no less a person than the Mayor of Jerningham. He must have a high opinion of your taste.'

It was Susanna's turn to look puzzled. 'But of *course* we chose them!' she said. 'I am longing to see the name on the board, though, aren't you, Papa?'

21

'The name? Ah yes, the name of the park.' He smiled at her. 'Have you been allowed to choose that too?'

'Now you are teasing!' She shook her head impatiently. 'It is not everybody that has a park named after them.'

'The Queen has a number of them,' he reminded her. 'There must be hundreds scattered about the cities and country towns of our land, not counting those in our possessions abroad. But perhaps this one is to be called the Jubilee Park for a change.' They were silent and he went on peevishly, 'I can see no reason why it should *not* be called the Jubilee Park! If one can believe the English newspapers there are Jubilee drinking-troughs and fountains springing up everywhere—an American has even presented one to Stratford-on-Avon—and Jubilee museums and libraries and orphanages abound. Therefore why not another Jubilee Park?'

'You are teasing again,' Susanna said. 'Oh yes then, it is to be called a Jubilee Park, and the statue inside the gates is to be of Queen Victoria herself!'

'With a small crown on her head over a lace veil and the sceptre gripped in her hand as if she would like to thump somebody with it!' he finished for her, and she laughed and he laughed with her. And as he did so the expression on her face suddenly altered. The laughter died and fright took its place. She pushed back her chair and got up.

'I don't feel very well,' she said, her face white. 'I think I'll go to my room—if you don't mind.' And she almost ran from the room.

'It's excitement,' Dinah said, frowning at the Admiral to take no notice. 'I will go upstairs after her and tuck her up in bed. She has been on wires all day.'

She hurried out of the room and up the stairs after her niece and helped her to get into bed, although

22

Susanna told her that she was well able to manage for herself.

'You can come down to dinner if you feel better, darling,' she said, stooping to kiss her before she left her. Susanna turned her face away.

'I'd rather have a tray brought to me here,' she said feebly. 'I feel—rather sick.'

'Then you shall have your meal in bed. Mrs. Beswick will send you up something nice and light.' And Dinah went away and left her.

When she was alone Susanna got up and went over to the window and sat there for a few moments looking out at the dripping trees in the park. The rain had ceased and a pale light was spreading towards the west, the dark clouds outlined in silver.

'When he laughed,' she whispered, 'his nose wrinkled. He isn't Papa. He is Uncle Will. But why is he here? And what can have happened to Papa?' And then another thought came, confirming the truth of it. 'Bruce knew! Clever old dog—he knew he wasn't his master and he tried to tell us. But why has Uncle Will come instead of Papa? Can he have come to tell us—that he is dead?'

.   .   .   .   .

Far from being dead the Admiral was at that moment seated in a fiacre in Paris on his way to catch the 7.15 overnight train to Marseilles, and his mind was far away from his family and his daughter, while if he gave his brother another thought it was with an amused wonder as to how he would carry the thing through.

'A schoolboy's trick,' Will had said. 'You cannot be serious. I should be discovered as an impostor at once.'

'But I *am* serious, Will,' his twin assured him. 'Des-

23

perately. And it is no schoolboy's trick. I cannot explain any more than that. But you will have to trust me and go.'

It had not occurred to him that Will would refuse to impersonate him at Waveney, and he was right. Will had never refused him anything in his life.

3

'Is there anything wrong?' asked Will Farebrother when Dinah returned.

'Nothing except excitement,' she told him serenely. 'She is at a difficult age—our Susie. I must tell you in confidence that she is always imagining herself to be in love. Not long ago it was the sculptor—Mr. Scaravicini —but fortunately that passed off. You remember I told you in one of my letters that he did the park statue here at Waveney, using one of the old coach-houses for the purpose? And of course as it was to be a statue of her papa Susie was in and out of the coach-house all the time, giving old Trot the slip, naughty girl, while pretending to tell Mr. Scaravicini how to carve out your face. He *was* a fascinating man, I suppose, to a young girl, but I was thankful when the statue was finished and a brewer's dray and steam engine arrived one morning to remove it to the park. I expect you saw it covered with tarpaulin there?'

'I did.' So that was it—a statue of John. Then the name of the park must be something to do with the family. He remembered that the bit of land where the park had been laid out had always belonged to Waveney, and it had never been any use—a bare bit of scrub. No doubt John had been glad to part with it to the town for a park. But why didn't he tell him before he left Paris? All he said was, 'And then there's the park to open and that damned statue to be unveiled.'

25

Naturally as it was the year of the Golden Jubilee he had thought it was something to do with the old queen. And who was old Trot, for goodness' sake? A horse? A groom?

As he pondered about it Dinah continued almost as if she had read his mind, 'I am so glad that Mrs. Somerton has found a nice situation for dear old Trot. Susie is past the age for governesses now and in any case Trot was no use except for making her practise the piano and her singing, and for translating French—which the little madam would get out of if she could. She complained that all the French books that Miss Bentley chose for her reading were so deadly dull, but I believe Mrs. Somerton would not hear of her girls reading French novels—though I do not suppose they would have harmed Susie very much.'

'I do not suppose so either. Zola perhaps might have been a little near the bone for her, but I can think of several others that she might have found amusing.'

Dinah looked surprised. 'I did not know that you could speak French, John?' she said. 'Let alone read it!'

'I've picked up a smattering in my travels,' he said quickly. 'You were saying about Miss Trot?'

'Oh yes. The Somertons will give up their governess soon, as Ella is out and Maud is coming out at Christmas. I believe the Bishop intends to treat Miss Bentley very handsomely when she leaves, giving her enough to set up a little school of her own in Jerningham, but of course we cannot afford to do anything like that for Trot. I did not know what to do about her, because you could not pension her off as you would an old servant, and find her a place in the Waveney almshouses. She is a gentlewoman, after all. I wished I could find some kindly old lady in need of a companion, but the only one I knew was your old Aunt Clara, and since she

26

lost her money she has been like a wasp and utterly
unreasonable in her demands. The last time she came to
stay at Waveney—which was last summer—she drove
us all nearly demented. So I knew she would be no good
for Trot.'

She paused, while he wondered why his Aunt Clara
had lost her money, and then she continued: 'Fortunately, as I said, Mrs. Somerton has come to the
rescue—not in the Palace, of course—but with a newcomer, a Mrs. Pontypool at Wentley Parva, who has a
delicate girl. I think it is a post that should suit Trot
very well. She left us last week, but there has not
been time yet to hear how she is settling down.'

There appeared to have been a new bishop in Jerningham since he was last in Waveney, the name Somerton
being new to him. But that did not worry him. He said
cautiously, trying to discover what he could without
betraying the fact that he had not known she had lost
her money, 'How is Aunt Clara managing?'

Dinah folded her lips tightly. She had a nice mouth,
he thought, but not when she pinched it up like that.

'Considering that she never intended to leave you a
penny, John, and that she openly boasted that it was
all to go to Will, and yet it is entirely due to *your* generosity that she is able to continue living in her house in
Putney, she does not show much gratitude. She still
seems to take it as her right that she will be invited to
Waveney every summer to be an active thorn in our
sides for a month or more.'

'She was always an unpredictable old lady,' Will said.

'If she were kinder and gentler I would not mind so
much,' added Dinah. 'You would have thought when
the bank failed and she lost everything except her
house, furniture and the clothes on her back, she might
have been more humbled in her outlook on life. But not
a bit of it. She is more evil-tempered than ever.'

27

So the bank had failed and her fortune with it.

'That is possibly why she has survived,' Will pointed out, smiling. 'A gentler soul would have gone down under such a blow and never risen again. But not Aunt Clara. She has always been a fighter.'

'You said that as if you admired her. Quite a new departure, John!'

'I only know what Will has told me about her,' he assured her hastily.

'Yes, of course, that dissolute brother of yours saw a great deal of her when he was at the art school in London. She is still devoted to him, in fact she did nothing but sing his praises when she was here last year— saying how clever he was and how unselfseeking. I was tired of the sound of his name by the time she left.'

'I'm afraid Will has never been any good,' he agreed wickedly, giving in to the impulse to tease her. 'You know what these artists are when they get to Paris.' And then, as Dinah drew down her mouth again in a way that made him want to laugh, he went on, 'I'm afraid my—dissolute brother lives in a manner that would shock you.'

'Then I'm sure I do not want to hear about it.' And then curiosity got the better of her and she added: 'I suppose he lives as we are told most artists live—in a bare attic that he calls a studio?'

'How did you guess? It is indeed a large bare attic at the top of a seedy house in the Quartier Latin. Bare floor with a model's platform in the middle of it, a smell of paint, an easel, loaves of bread and bottles of wine mixed up with jars of paint brushes.'

'And what was he painting when you went to see him there?'

'A picture of a girl with a gipsy's face.' And here in spite of himself a smile touched his mouth as he re-

28

membered his little model Francine. Dinah saw the smile and frowned.

'I hope she wasn't—' She broke off, unable to continue.

'She was clothed,' he reassured her. 'Decency had been observed!'

'He left some paintings of his in the old nursery. Susie loves them—and I will admit that some show great promise. But I cannot understand why he did not stay in London after he finished at the school in Charlotte Street. He might have been accepted by the Royal Academy School and had the benefit of the advice of some of our leading artists.'

'Perhaps he did not like the way they painted,' said Will mildly, but he sounded amused and she thought he was laughing at her and smiled unwillingly.

'I do not care for the new French art at all,' she said. 'Mrs. Taverner has a book of engravings and she showed me a picture in it of a whole lot of people with their umbrellas up. "Now, my dear," she said, "what is there to praise in that? Anybody with an idea of drawing could paint a lot of umbrellas!"'

'But not perhaps as Renoir painted them,' Will said, and then stopped, wondering how much his brother knew about painting. Dinah, however, only laughed.

'I can see that Will has been trying to teach you his trade, but I don't suppose he will succeed very well. Did you tell him that the only pictures you ever liked were of ships and horses?'

'I think he knows that by this time,' Will said. He liked her when she laughed: quite suddenly she became a different person altogether. He thought, 'If only she could lose that starchy manner and that look of disapproval, how nice she might be.' He seemed to remember, however, that the Woodcocks had been a strait-laced lot.

She folded her work and put it away in her work-box and got up and said she must join Susie. 'It has been an exciting day for us all,' she told him, smiling. 'And I'm sure you will be glad to get to your bed. Dorothea and her father will be here to add their welcome to ours tomorrow. They refused to intrude on your first evening at home.' She held out her hand. 'Good night, John, and sleep well. It is good to have you home again.' There was a touch of sadness in the smile that accompanied the words and it haunted him a little as he went up to his room.

Jobson was waiting for him, but he sent him away to his bed. Before they had parted in Paris, after the whirlwind arrangements the Admiral had made for them both, he had told his brother to take with him the writing desk that had always travelled with him at sea.

'Browse through the things in it at your leisure,' he said. 'You are at liberty to read any private correspondence you may find there as well as the business letters. It may help you when you meet people you don't know. Although we are still as alike as two peas in a pod and when Jobson has trimmed your beard to my imperial and cut your hair and put you into some of my clothes, I'll swear there's not a soul in Waveney or Jerningham who will know the difference.' He had clapped him on the shoulder with his usual enthusiasm. 'I need a red herring, my dear Will, and you are the one to provide it for me.'

'I have been called many things in my time,' he had replied wryly, 'but never a red herring.'

John had only laughed, however, and on his way to the door had paused by the easel to say, 'I like your gipsy. I can almost smell her rags!' and he had gone on his way, and although Will had wanted to call him back, knowing that there must be hundreds of objections to his mad scheme, he could not think of any valid ones until now.

Now they crowded in on him thick and fast. He had not known about Trot, for instance, who turned out to be neither a horse nor a groom, but a governess. He had not known about the new bishop's name, nor about the wretched park, whose name he had still to discover. And who was this Dorothea, and her father, who were descending upon him tomorrow?

And Scaravacini, whom he had met and heartily disliked in Italy—he could only hope that the man had gone back there long ago.

Will Farebrother did not like reading other people's letters, and he started on the business ones first, opening one in particular that looked as if it had been addressed by a lawyer's clerk. It was not from a lawyer, however, it was from the manager of the bank in Jerningham, and it surprised and shocked him not a little.

He wrote to tell Admiral Sir John Farebrother that he was anxious to see him as soon as possible after his return home, as he had some excellent news to impart about the mortgage on the Waveney property.

Will read it with dismay. A mortgage on Waveney— but why? His brother had never been extravagant and was seldom at home to run up large bills, while from what he had observed that evening his family seemed content with the simplest fare. Who could have encumbered the estate, then? There had seemed to be no difficulty in finding the ten thousand pounds that had been his own legacy when their father died. And then he remembered what Dinah had said about his brother's kindness to their Aunt Clara. It was as natural to his carelessly generous nature to pay his brother his legacy, however much the estate was in debt, as it was to allow

31

the old lady a sufficient income to keep her in her Putney house.

He felt suddenly guilty. All his life he had been thankful to a Providence that had made his twin the elder by two hours and therefore heir to Waveney. He had been free to go his own way and to paint outside the restrictions that his father put upon them both. Sir Roger had been a real martinet: he had never forgiven his younger son for refusing to go into the Navy with his twin. It was a life for a man, he told him, and would soon knock all this nonsense of painting and art out of his head.

It was their Aunt Clara who had come to his rescue, paying the fees for the art school in Charlotte Street when his father refused to do so, and in fact any success he might have had was entirely due to her. And yet it was his brother who had repaid her for her kindness.

It seemed that he might have left more than one burden for his twin to carry single-handed, and it was no excuse to say that he had not known such burdens existed. He determined to go and see the bank manager the following day and discover how the Waveney accounts stood without being discovered himself.

He did not trouble to read any other letters in the desk before he went to bed, but the bed was strange and he did not sleep well, and directly it was light he dressed and went out walking in the grounds, turning towards the walnut avenue that led as a short cut to Waveney village.

It was a fine morning after the rain of the day before and in the ordinary course of events his artist's eye would have rested with delight on the soft English colouring of the park and the trees in all their different shades of green and gold.

But he was too worried to enjoy anything. There was a fallen tree-trunk halfway down the avenue and he

32

spread his waterproof cape over it and sat down, poking at the wet turf with the point of his cane and with John's deer-stalker pushed to the back of his head.

And then suddenly he saw somebody hurrying down the avenue towards him from the direction of the house. and as she drew near he saw that it was Susanna.

4

Susanna, too, had slept badly that night. She heard her aunt come upstairs to bed and half hoped, half dreaded that she might come in to tell her that she had made the same discovery about her Uncle Will. But Dinah only went on into her room and Susanna was left wide-eyed to be a prey to all sorts of imaginary fears.

As it grew light she could not stay in bed any longer. She got up and dressed, washing her hands and face in cold water and brushing out the tangles in her thick chestnut hair, combing out the naturally curly fringe in front and twisting the rest into a knot at the back of her head.

It was about half past six as she opened her door and looked out on to the wide landing. A housemaid was sweeping the stairs with a soft brush, making so little noise that it was not possible to hear her behind a closed door, and somewhere in the direction of her aunt's small sitting-room she could hear the sound of a grate being as noiselessly cleaned. Until the end of May fires were lighted in the Manor rooms at dusk.

Susanna fetched her jacket and hat and went downstairs, to the surprise of the housemaid, who, however, only smiled at her and told her that the Admiral had beaten her. 'He was up and out a good half-hour ago,' she said.

'I wonder which way he went?' Susanna felt that she must find her uncle at once and ask him to his face why he was there in the Admiral's shoes.

'I see him through the big window as I was coming up the stairs with my dustpan and brush,' the girl said. 'Looked like he was making for the avenue.'

There was only one avenue at Waveney. 'I will see if he is there,' Susanna said, and ran on down the stairs and let herself out by the library windows. Perryman had already unbarred the shutters and folded them back and it was easy to open them and be outside in a flash.

The young golden green of the walnut trees formed two lines of colour against the emerald of the new summer's grass. After the rain the sky was a tender early-morning blue, and in the grass the summer flowers were spreading, daisy heads and dandelions and patches of buttercups, beginning to open up after the soaking of the day before. She soon caught sight of her uncle, seated on the fallen tree-trunk. He was staring in front of him, frowning a little as if there was something on his mind, but he looked up as she approached and got up quickly, taking off his hat and stooping to kiss her.

'Why, Susanna,' he said, 'I did not expect you to be astir so early.'

'I came to find you,' she said simply.

'Share my cape.' He spread it out wider on the log. 'This old tree is soaking wet. And what about your slippers, child? Aren't they wet through?'

'Never mind about my slippers,' she said, too impatient to be polite. 'And I don't think I'll sit down if you don't mind, Uncle Will. I want to know why you are here in Papa's place, please?'

He looked at her quickly, and she wondered if he was going to lie to her and try to bluff it out, but after a moment's silence he said quietly, with rather a wry little smile, 'I told your father it would be no good. What we did as schoolboys is no longer possible now that we are grown men. But you know what he is like

35

when he gets an idea into his head: he must have his own way.'

'He is all right, then? He is not ill?' Relief sounded in her voice and he glanced at her face and saw the fright in it for the first time.

'My dear child,' he said tenderly, 'did you think something had happened to him?'

She nodded. 'I thought you might have come to tell us that he was dead,' she said in a shaking voice. He put his arm round her quickly and drew her down to sit beside him on the waterproof cape, and apologised for having worried her so much.

'I did not think of this, and neither did he,' he said. 'Tell me, Susanna, when did you discover that I was not your father? Was it at tea last evening? There was something I did—or said—that told you?'

'It was your laugh.' She told him of her discovery when she was a child. 'I had to find some difference between you,' she said. 'And I did.'

'I said he was making a mistake to underrate his daughter's powers of perception. He wouldn't listen to me, of course. He said, "Nonsense, my dear fellow, she was only seven years old when she saw you last. I guarantee she will not remember anything about you." But I thought seven-year-olds could be very observant, and you see I was right.' His cheerful voice and manner reassured her. They were just having a joke, perhaps.

'Is that what it is?' she asked, puzzled. 'Just a joke?'

'No, my dear, it is not a joke.' He frowned, trying to make up his mind as to how much he should tell her. But it had all been done in such a hurry that he had not had time to discuss with John what he should say if he were found out. He went on slowly, choosing his words, 'When your father landed at Southampton Jobson brought him a letter that had come for him here.'

'Yes. It was marked "Important" and looked very

official, so we thought he ought to have it without delay.'

'That letter told him to report to the Admiralty as soon as possible, and so he went there before coming home. They asked him to undertake an important mission: he could not tell me much about it, except that he had to travel incognito and that he would be away about a fortnight.'

'But that means he will not be here to open the park?'

'Precisely. And that is why I am here—in his shoes. He did not want to disappoint the good people of Jerningham.' It sounded a lame excuse, but it was better for her to think that the unveiling of the statue and the opening of the park were the reasons for his presence there than that, as the Admiral had hinted, there might be danger to her father if his absence abroad were known.

Susanna was no fool, however. She shot him a droll glance from her hazel eyes and said that she did not believe him for one moment.

'The Admiralty has plenty of other people to send on their mysterious missions,' she told him. 'No, Uncle Will. Papa has some mission of his own in Paris and he does not want anybody to know about it—especially perhaps Mrs. Taverner, and Miss Dudley and Dorothea.'

'And who might those three ladies be?'

'You will find out soon enough. But Papa is safe from me. I shall not ask any questions.' She laughed and got to her feet. 'I'm hungry. It must be nearly breakfast-time and Aunt Dinah will be wondering what has become of us.' And then as he got up and began to walk with her towards the house, relieved that she appeared to connect her father's absence with some romantic assignment in Paris, she slipped her hand into his arm and said, 'Papa is coming home soon, I suppose?'

37

'He expects to be back at the end of a fortnight, I believe.'

'In time for my coming-out ball. I hope you will stay for it?'

'My dear, how can I? I trust by that time this—little joke—will be over and I shall be back in Paris.' He asked her to keep the whole thing a secret for her father's sake and she nodded. He wondered who had told her of the nature of the establishments that her father might have visited in London and elsewhere when he had been on shore leave in the past. No man would regard such adventures with any surprise: the Admiral's wife had been dead for a number of years and he was a man with tastes that could not be totally subdued by the vigorous exercise he took at home. But it appeared that such knowledge, while it might shock her aunt to the core, had not disturbed the young woman beside him in the least. He thought that probably there were many things Susanna had learned as she grew up, not from her aunt nor from the governess at the Palace, but possibly through the careless talk of old servants, or from the overheard chat of grooms and gamekeepers. It seemed that she might have been left very much on her own at Waveney. The next moment she surprised him by saying that there was only one person she thought she should tell and that was her aunt. 'I promise you,' she added hastily, as he made a movement of protest, 'she is the most dependable person in the world. When she realises what has happened—however much she may disapprove of Papa's activities—she will not breathe a word to anyone. Whenever I have tried to talk to her about—Papa—in the past she has always said, "My dear, I don't think we should discuss your father's private business, do you?" She is so intensely loyal, you see.'

He did see, and was agreeably impressed, while at

the same time he agreed that neither of them could deceive her aunt with a quiet conscience.

When he mentioned at breakfast that morning, however, that he intended driving into Jerningham to see the bank manager, Susanna said at once that she would go with him, and Dinah remarked that she was sure Mr. Forest would be glad to see him.

Will did not think the manager's signature had resembled the name of 'Forest', although it might have been almost anything in contrast to the beautiful calligraphy of the letter itself, but Susanna came swiftly to his rescue by remarking casually how much they admired Mr. Forest's handwriting, and that Mr. Peppercorn was fortunate to have inherited a head clerk who wrote so well. She went on innocently, 'Mr. Peppercorn was not manager of the bank when Papa was here last, was he, Aunt Di? He came soon after Papa went back to sea I think?'

'Yes. He has been in Jerningham nearly two years. He will be pleased to make your acquaintance, John.'

Will caught a flash of mischief in Susanna's eyes and smiled in return. Dinah glanced at her thoughtfully. There was a demure look about her this morning that did not escape her, and she wondered if she were up to mischief, although it was of course only natural that she should wish to be with her father that morning. But she could not help remembering that lately, when they visited Jerningham to carry out small errands of shopping, they usually managed to meet Captain Sloane, quite by accident, as he bought ties in the High Street. He seemed to be a young man with very little else to do.

.   .   .   .   .

Captain Sloane was a nephew of the Honourable Iris Dudley and had stayed with her on and off during the past hunting season. He rode well and Miss Dudley had

39

supplied him with a couple of hunters so that he could follow the hounds, and when hunting was finished he still managed to fit in frequent visits to his aunt. It was extraordinary, Dinah thought, how much time a young officer could give to pleasure when there was no war to demand his services in other fields.

For a time Dinah had thought that Ella Somerton had been the attraction that drew him to Jerningham, encouraged by Miss Dudley because the Bishop was a rich man and she was anxious for her nephew to win for himself a rich bride. He was an extravagant young man. Lately, however, when they had met him on their shopping expeditions, he had not been accompanied by Miss Somerton, and the way he had looked and spoken to Susanna made her aunt think uneasily that he might be considering the Admiral's daughter as his future bride instead of the plain Ella. After all, to those who did not know the circumstances of the case, Susanna was heiress to Waveney. Captain Sloane might see himself as the Admiral's son-in-law, well established at the Grange, perhaps, living off the estate very comfortably, with hunters in his stables and an almost unlimited credit with the tradespeople in Jerningham. For a young man whose finances were always at a low ebb it would be an attractive prospect.

Dinah did not want her beloved niece to marry a poor man. Although through force of circumstances she had brought her up frugally and to practise economy, like making her own dresses and trimming her own hats, and mending clothes and gloves and stockings, and Mrs. Beswick had taught her how to make preserves and pickles and jellies and all the things that a future little housekeeper should know, they were all things to which she did not take kindly and a sovereign in her pocket still meant to Susanna a sovereign to be spent.

40

As they drove into Jerningham together, Will asked his niece when she intended telling her aunt about her father's little joke. She shook her head, laughing. 'Later. Aunt Dinah has to be prepared for anything like that.' Her eyes were dancing, however, and he said, much amused:

'I believe you are enjoying the lark as much as your father is!'

'Well, you must admit it is rather fun!' She gave his hand an affectionate squeeze. 'I thought I had better come with you in case you meet any of Papa's old cronies in the town and you won't know them, but they will fancy they know you, and that might be disastrous.'

He gave the little hand in his a warm pressure. 'Bless you, what a wise little creature you are. But when will you tell your aunt?'

She laughed again at the expression on his face. 'Don't look alarmed! She won't eat you—though she may scold, mind. But she will never betray Papa—that I can promise you.'

On arriving at the bank, she accompanied him into the building, and as the grey-haired clerk came forward to welcome them, she said quickly, 'Mr. Forest, I know you are as glad as I am to see the Admiral home again.'

'I am indeed, miss.' He beamed at Will. 'We have been looking forward to your return, Sir John. May I express the feelings of us all when I say welcome home?'

'Thank you, Forest.' Susanna left him, saying that she would wait for him in the carriage, and he followed the clerk to the manager's office, a sanctum that he had never entered in his life, preferring to keep his own account in a London bank.

It was going to be a difficult interview, but if he played his cards correctly he thought he might be able to discover all he wanted to know. He wondered how much Dinah Woodcock knew about the state of affairs at Waveney and he wondered too with a feeling of apprehension what she would say when Susanna told her about her father's joke. He had dismissed her the night before as being austere, and the slight attempt she had made to join in the conversation at breakfast had confirmed him in that opinion. He was not to know that Dinah's thoughts were entirely with the luncheon to which the Ashworths had been invited, and if the claret she had ordered from the wine merchant the week before would suit the tastes of the gentlemen. Not for the first time she wished that her brother-in-law would write to the wine merchant himself and order what he wanted before coming home. It was years since the Manor had had a wine cellar and the Admiral always said that a woman knew nothing about wines. And from the way Perryman had turned up his nose at the claret she did not think it could be very good. She could be quite sure, moreover, that if it were not good the Admiral would not hesitate to tell her so in front of their friends.

She hoped that the Admiral would get married again now that he was home for good, and she hoped with all her heart that he would choose Dorothea Ashworth when the time came.

Dear Dorothea, with her kind, generous nature, and her charming, tender face, would be the nicest possible mistress of Waveney, and Susanna would love her as a stepmamma. And yet, mused Dinah, always so ready to worry, would she attempt to control Susanna, or would she let her go her own way, however many penniless young officers she fell in love with? It was a question to which there was no answer, and a question which only the Admiral could settle now that he was home.

5

Mr. Peppercorn was a pleasant-faced man in his early fifties, with shrewd eyes and a rather formal manner that revealed nothing of his feelings, if indeed, Will thought, managers of banks could allow themselves feelings when dealing with their customers. He unbent sufficiently, however, to add his welcome to his clerk's.

'You received my letter, Sir John?' he said, bringing a chair forward for him by his desk. 'I addressed it to Marseilles.'

'And that is why I am here,' Will said blandly. 'You said in that letter that you had some good news for me about the Waveney mortgage?'

'Yes, Sir John. I am happy to tell you that the mortgage on your property no longer exists, thanks to the efforts of your agent, Mr. Homer, and yourself. Both land and house are now free from debt, and I would like to add that when I last saw Mr. Homer he told me how greatly he had been helped by the economies of Miss Woodcock in your household. There is now no need for the sacrifice of your timber, as I believe was mooted when you discussed the matter with my predecessor when you were last at home.'

Having had no idea that the Waveney timber had been threatened. Will said he was glad to hear it.

'The mortgage was, of course, taken up many years before I came here, so that I know little of the circumstances that made it necessary,' went on Mr. Peppercorn. 'But I understand it was due to the thoughtlessness of others that you inherited an estate so heavily encumbered. I believe even the forty thousand pounds you had been led to expect no longer existed?'

As this was as much news to Will as the timber felling, he bent his head and made no reply, and the manager went on:

'I understand, too, that none of your employees were dismissed and that you continued to do the usual repairs on your tenants' farms and dwelling houses, added to which you paid your brother the ten thousand legacy that had been left to him in your father's will, and that you have been paying Mrs. Clara Duncombe an income of five hundred pounds a year. I presume that you wish this to continue?'

'Certainly.'

'I believe my predecessor said there was some talk of the old lady coming to live at Waveney, but that you did not wish to consider it?'

'She would not have liked it at all,' said Will positively. 'She is a very independent old lady.'

'Then naturally the income must be paid to her still. I will see to it for you. And in the meantime the deeds of Waveney are still in the strong-room here under lock and key, only with this difference: they are now your property alone, and the bank has no claim on them. May I repeat, Sir John, how happy this makes me, and to add that if we can assist you at any time I shall be at your disposal?'

'Thank you. I am much obliged to you.' Will left feeling that he had learned most of what he wanted to know without having to probe very hard, and he was mortified and dismayed at what he had discovered.

He found Susanna sitting in the carriage outside, talking to a young man at the carriage door. He was a good-looking young man and Susanna was very animated and looking extremely pretty. The young man's

44

eyes were on her face and neither of them saw him until the groom came to open the door for him and Susanna's friend had to move.

'Oh!' she said, going rather pink. 'I don't think you have met Papa, have you, Captain Sloane?'

'I would have known you anywhere, Sir John,' said Captain Sloane with heartening assurance. 'Mr. Scaravicini has caught your likeness remarkably well, considering that he had only a photograph to copy.'

Will studied him thoughtfully. 'So you have seen the statue, have you?' he said.

'Yes, sir.'

'Ella and Maud Somerton came to gather primroses in our woods just before Easter,' Susanna told him. 'And Captain Sloane came with them in the Bishop's carriage. After tea I took them down to the coach-house to see the statue and they all thought it very like you.'

So the Bishop's daughters had also seen the darned thing. He wondered who else had been taken to the coach-house to see it. The young man said goodbye reluctantly to Susanna and the carriage moved on down the High Street.

'Isn't he wonderful?' said Susanna ecstatically.

'I beg your pardon?' Will, whose mind had gone back to the timber that might have been felled at Waveney, was mystified, and she gave his arm a little shake.

'Captain Sloane,' she said, adding softly, 'His name is Frank. I think it is the loveliest name for a man, don't you?'

'I haven't thought about it,' he said. 'But I will give it my consideration now if you wish.'

Again came that impatient shake of his arm. 'You are teasing again!' And then she took her hand away and sighed. 'Aunt Dinah says Papa will never let me marry him because I'm too young. But Mamma was only eighteen when she married Papa and nobody said she was too young, did they?'

'Well, I don't know about that. They may have said so. From what I remember of your father's wedding there was a strong atmosphere of disapproval on the Woodcock side of it.' She made a face and after a moment he went on: 'Has the young man any money?'

'He has his pay.'

'Which would feed a sparrow. But has he nothing besides? A rich father, for instance?'

'No, his father is not well off at all. He is staying with his aunt, Miss Dudley, who is a lord's daughter and very rich.'

'Ah then no doubt he has expectations in that direction?'

'Oh no. I mean she is very pleased to have him to stay for the hunting season, and to escort her to balls and that sort of thing. But Aunt Dinah and I think she really wants to find him a rich wife, and that is why she keeps throwing poor Ella Somerton at his head.'

'Why do you say "poor" Ella?'

'Well, you see, she is rather plain, and she has been out for two seasons and both of them she has spent with an aunt in London—Mrs. Somerton says she is "one of the leading London hostesses" but I don't believe it for a moment. And whatever she may be she hasn't got Ella married yet or anywhere near it.'

'And yet Miss Somerton must be a prize, must she not, if Miss Dudley is trying to win her for her nephew?' Will's voice was dry and Susanna shot a shrewd look at him.

'People say that the Bishop is going to settle a lot of money on Ella and Maud when they marry,' she said slowly. Her face clouded for a moment and then, like quicksilver, it was brimming with laughter. 'A man will need some sort of bribe to marry Ella.'

46

He did not smile. He said gently, 'My love, if Miss Somerton is a friend of yours, that is scarcely a kind thing to say.'

She flushed and bit her lip. 'I know,' she said penitently. 'I am a beast. The Somertons *are* my friends and they have been so kind to me. But—' she broke off and he thought he was able to fill the gap.

'You do not wish Captain Sloane to be interested in Miss Somerton perhaps?'

'I am in love with him,' she said simply. 'Uncle Will, I don't mind if he is poor. It will be fun to be poor—with him.' Her pretty eyes sought his. 'Money is not important, is it, if you love each other?'

'It depends upon how you have been brought up,' he said cautiously.

'I believe you are going to side with Aunt Dinah,' she said chagrined.

'I am siding with nobody,' he replied, smiling.

'Of course,' she said thoughtfully, 'in the place of my father you could give your consent to an engagement?'

'Of course I would do nothing of the sort.'

'Not even if I threatened to tell on you to your friends?'

'Why, you wicked little thing!' He turned his head and saw that her face was full of laughter. 'If you ever did a thing like that, my child—in your father's place, I would put you over my knee and give you a beating.'

'Papa has never beaten me in his life.'

'That anyone could guess.'

'Do you think I'm so spoilt? Aunt Dinah says I am.' She sounded rather complacent about it.

'Your aunt is perfectly right.'

'But you must admit that Frank is very handsome?'

'If looks were all I'd say he would make an ideal

47

husband, but unfortunately more than looks are necessary for a happy marriage.'

'Now how can you know anything about it? You have never been married, have you?'

'Never.' He sounded so satisfied that she laughed again and then he added, 'There must be many more young men in the neighbourhood who would be equally attractive as husbands, Susanna.'

'Nobody,' she said. It was at that moment that a man driving a spirited mare harnessed to a dog-cart with a groom up beside him approached them from the Waveney road. On seeing them, he lifted his hat to Will, bowed coolly to Susanna and went on, the mare being in no mood to linger.

'Who was that?' asked Will, interested.

'That's Mr. Royde, our neighbour,' she said. 'A most detestable man.'

'Is he married?'

'No. His sister who is a widow—Lady Sare—lives at Royde Park with him. She is nice and Aunt Dinah and I like her very much. But her brother—' words failed her and her uncle laughed.

'If he is the owner of Royde Park surely he is worth cultivating? He would be an eligible husband for some lucky girl.'

'Believe, me, Uncle Will, no girl married to Mr. Royde would be lucky. She would be the most downtrodden, snubbed, miserable wretch in the world.'

'I am sorry you find the present owner of Royde so unlikable. I remember his father very well and he was a kindly man. He died fairly recently, I believe?'

'Yes. The doctors said it was peritonitis—whatever that may mean. He suffered a great deal of pain, poor man. Lady Sare was living at Royde then—her husband was killed in the Zulu war.'

'And you would not like to be Mrs. Royde?'

48

'That I would not. Frank may be desperately poor but I love him and I would not marry anybody else if he was as rich as Croesus with a dozen Royde Parks.' She broke off with a sigh. 'I do hope Papa will like him.'

He wondered if Captain Sloane's pursuit of Miss Farebrother would be quite so ardent if he had known that her father was only just out of debt to the bank to the tune of what must have been well over forty thousand pounds. Worldly wise after his years abroad, with a knowledge of the French way of arranging marriages and comparing them in his mind with the marriages often arranged—though always said to be love-matches—between families in England, he had little faith in marrying for love, and thought it unlikely that such a state of affairs really existed. Cynically he turned it over in his mind, leaving Susanna to dream of her gallant captain until the carriage reached Waveney and the prospect of luncheon.

Two figures were walking across the park in front of them, however, and as she saw them Susanna gave an exclamation of dismay.

'The Ashworths!' she cried. 'I forgot all about them. They are coming to luncheon and I meant to tell you who they were—and I quite forgot. Oh dear, what will you do? Captain Ashworth is one of Papa's oldest friends—they were midshipmen together.'

'Keep your head,' said Will in a low voice. 'What does your father call him?'

'Jack. It isn't his real name—it's Frederick—but he always has called him Jack. I don't know why.'

'And the girl with him is his daughter?'

'Yes. That's Dorothea.'

'Does your father call her Dorothea or Miss Ash-worth?'

'Oh, Dorothea. We all call her Dorothea. She is our

49

greatest friend. We are hoping—Aunt Dinah and I—that she will marry Papa.'

'I see. Does she know that?'

'Of course not.'

'I am glad of that.' It seemed that in England they had not given up the habit of arranging marriages either, but he was relieved to find that he would not be expected to pay court to Captain Ashworth's daughter. He would lie on John's behalf, he would let Jobson dress him up in the Admiral's clothes, he would do his best to imitate his brother's voice and ways, but he utterly refused to take any hand in his love affairs.

The Ashworths were overtaken, the carriage stopped and was sent on to the stables, while Will and his niece joined their guests.'

'Welcome home, Sir John!' Dorothea put out her hand to take his. 'You must be glad to get home to Waveney at last.'

'Yes, it's good to see you home again, John, and for good this time.' Captain Ashworth gripped his hand in his turn, examining his face with a pair of extremely sharp grey eyes. 'Miss Susanna's happy, I know, to think that her father will not be going away again. Hey, Susanna?'

'I am indeed,' Susanna said, smiling.

'We'll have to start those games of chess again,' went on the Captain. 'Dinah has been giving me a game now and then in your absence, but we have both missed your games, haven't we, Dorothea?'

'We have.' Dorothea walked on with Susanna ahead of the two men and began to ask what time her father had arrived the day before and if he had had a good journey and poor Susanna answered at random, stretching her ears to discover what the men behind them were talking about. She wondered if her uncle could play chess, and presently she turned and said, 'The winter is the time for chess, Captain Ashworth. You mustn't take Papa away from me in the summer, when he has only just arrived.'

'I promise you I shall not do that,' he said smiling.

'We will keep our games of chess for later on, Jack,' Will said hastily and added, 'Will you not let me carry that basket for you, Dorothea?'

'It's a very small one, thank you, Admiral, and very precious. Too precious to allow out of my keeping. It contains a clutch of bantam's eggs that Dinah wanted. She says she has a broody that will sit on them but I think it is late in the year.'

'There is no accounting for broodies,' he said, and was about to launch into a description of a broody who had flown off her nest upsetting his easel into a duck pond years ago when he caught himself in time. He was the Admiral, he reminded himself, not his dissolute artist brother.

It seemed a very long day and he fancied that his niece was not enjoying their friends' company very much either. He tried to talk heartily about Waveney and country subjects—of which he knew very little— and avoided talking about the Admiral's last voyage— of which he knew nothing at all. If such visits between Waveney and the Grange were almost a daily occurrence he thought he would have to invent business to take him to London and keep him there until John came home, only visiting Jerningham to hand over the park and for the unveiling of the statue. He could not possibly keep up the pretence of being his brother in front of this astute man and his daughter.

After they had gone he went down to the stables and had the groom put a saddle on to a harmless old cob that the man told him was too old to throw him or

51

behave any way else than soberly. 'Honeysett told me you used to ride him a lot when you was home before, sir,' he added. 'Flash is his name because of the white flash on his forehead, but he's far from flashy by nature.'

The man was right. Flash was a sedate old thing and took him for a steady amble through the lanes, and though he was out for a couple of hours or more nowhere could he see any sign of poverty or neglect. Waveney showed every evidence of being a well-kept estate.

Somewhat reassured, he returned to the house to be greeted by Susanna with the news that she had told her aunt about the trick they were playing and she had not liked it at all.

.   .   .   .   .

As they walked home over the park Dorothea Ashworth said: 'Papa, is it my imagination, or was there something odd in the Admiral's manner—and in fact in himself, if it comes to that?'

'In what way did you think him odd, my dear?'

'I can't quite say what it was, but one missed his heartiness—he seemed subdued and unlike himself. And he is very much thinner. I wondered if he were ill?'

'He did seem distrait and unlike himself,' agreed her father, 'No doubt he was tired after his journey. I should not have said there was any need to go to Paris directly he arrived in England, just to see his brother. But there may have been business reasons for the visit, of course. I have heard a whisper now and then that the Waveney estates are hopelessly in debt, and I daresay the poor fellow may be wondering how he is going to manage now he is home again.'

'I did not think he seemed worried,' Dorothea said.

'As I said, I cannot put a finger on it—he was just different.'

'You're imagining things,' said her father, and then as a rabbit popped up in front of them, 'Oh, if I had my gun.'

'Poor bunny!' Dorothea said. 'What a bloodthirsty lot you men are!'

They said no more about it, but that night, after his daughter had retired to bed and the Captain sat smoking one last pipe before retiring himself, he thought over what she had said about his old friend.

John had certainly not been like himself at all. Usually he was full of his voyages and the places he had visited and the people who had entertained him there and any mutual friends he had met. This last voyage had been the China Station and he had not mentioned Sydney until Dorothea had asked him with an archness that should have made him throw back his head and laugh—and did not—if he had run across Mrs. Taverner there. The good lady had been visiting relations in Australia at the time that the Admiral's flagship had been in Sydney.

He had only said yes, he had seen her and she had brought him up-to-date news of Jerningham and immediately changed the subject to the question of repairs that Homer was having put in hand down at the Grange. Such behaviour was odd indeed.

It was after he had knocked out his pipe and was turning out the table lamp that a possible solution to the mystery offered itself and he stopped short before blowing out the lowered wicks, staring in front of him at the darkened room.

'They might have done a thing like that when they were schoolboys,' he thought. 'But not as grown men. And why should they? Did John not want to get home? In every letter he has said how much he was longing for

53

Waveney. But it was odd that he went to see his brother all the same. And it is like him to do it.' He chuckled, remembering the pranks they used to get up to when they were both lads on their first ship, and still smiling he blew out the lamp and went up to bed.

6

There was no doubt about it that Dinah was upset. During the whole of dinner she was ominously silent, and she remained silent until Susanna had gone up to bed. It was a most uncomfortable evening.

It was a chilly night and there was a good fire burning on the hearth, but whatever warmth was created there was quite insufficient to thaw the ice in Miss Woodcock's manner.

'Susanna has told me about this trick that you and John have played on us, Mr. Farebrother,' she said in her severest tone when they were alone together. 'And I must say that I am surprised and disgusted that two grown men should act in such a childish way. Why, in heaven's name, did you become a party to it?'

'Susanna told you perhaps that her father is engaged on a rather important mission?' he hazarded.

'Which I believe as little as she does,' she replied cuttingly. 'There is a woman in it, of course.'

'If there is I know nothing about it.' He told her of his brother's call at the Admiralty and how he was asked to perform the mission. 'He did not say what it was and I did not ask but I did not question its importance either. It was when he asked me to be his red herring here in Waveney that I began to think there might be danger in it—either to himself or to somebody else. He was very anxious that he should be thought to be here.'

'I suppose it was he then who sent that notice to the

Morning Post this morning?' said Dinah slowly.

'Was there a notice in it? About John?'

'Oh yes. It simply said that "one of the nation's heroes", Admiral Sir John Farebrother, arrived home at his country place, Waveney Manor, yesterday afternoon.'

'Possibly the Admiralty put it in. If so they were damned quick about it.'

'Whether John was telling the truth or not,' Dinah went on, 'I still think you are being stupid and childish to think you could ever carry such a thing through, and I imagine if you are found out things may be worse for John abroad—or wherever he may be. I thought you were unlike yourself when you arrived—that is to say, I thought John was unlike himself.' She broke off, confused, and then continued: 'You will be found out, of course. You must be. Susanna discovered who you were almost at once, and now she has told me I can see for myself how different you are from John. You are thinner, you haven't his manner, nor his voice. Why, you can hear John's voice from one end of the house to the other!'

'Yes, I'm afraid I never have had a very loud voice,' agreed Will humbly.

'The servants will soon know all about it too,' went on Dinah indignantly. 'If they don't know already.'

'Oh dear, am I as bad as all that?'

'Well, I suppose Jobson knows, doesn't he?'

'Of course. One cannot keep secrets—however important—from one's valet.'

'There you are then. It will get round. Bound to.' She sounded triumphant. 'Besides, you will make mistakes. You made one directly you set foot in the house yesterday. You said something to Mrs. Beswick about her preserves, and she picked you up at once. It was Mr. Will who liked her preserves, she told you.'

'Yes, that was bad,' he admitted. 'But for poor old John's sake I can but do my best.' He studied her face reflectively. 'And now that I have enlightened you as best I can, perhaps you will be so kind as to enlighten me about the Waveney property. I had no idea that there had ever been a mortgage on it until I saw the bank manager in Jerningham this morning. John said nothing of it in any of his letters and I was quite horrified when I heard about it. But it may be news to you too?'

She felt surprise and a touch of chagrin because she might have been misjudging him over the years.

'I will tell you what I can,' she said slowly. 'But John does not tell me everything and I do not like prying into his private concerns.'

'Do you know why Waveney became so encumbered in the first place? When I was here as a boy there was never any lack of money.'

'It was when your father died I believe that it was discovered. John was at home and after the funeral he found out how deeply the estate was in debt. Your father, he told me once, had always liked to live in an extravagant way—there was his house in London where he and your mother entertained a great deal when he was a Member of Parliament. Well, Members of Parliament are not paid for their services, are they? And they are expected to do a great deal of entertaining. In other words, they should be rich men. And, of course, Homer was not here then and the agent Sir Roger employed robbed him up hill and down dale.'

He could not help smiling at the homeliness of the expression and he thought what a nice woman she was under her starchy manner. He liked the direct honesty of her eyes and the firmness of her mouth.

'And I was in Italy at the time,' he said sadly, 'and unable to afford the journey home for the funeral. It

57

was so like John not to wish to trouble me with bad news. My legacy must have been an added burden to the estate.'

'He knew it was necessary to you,' she said. 'He always felt guilty, he told me once, because he had so much and you had so little. Two hours, he said, should never have given one twin a house and a fortune at the expense of the other.'

'A fortune?'

'It should have been so, if your father had been wise.' She began to fold her work. 'John said once that if he had not died when he did Waveney would have had to be sold.'

'At least now it is clear of debt,' he said.

'Clear of debt? Waveney?' The relief in her face made him wonder if he should not have left John to tell her himself. He said gently, 'I do not know how heavily he has encumbered himself with Aunt Clara, of course, beyond paying her five hundred a year?'

'That is the income he allows her, and she seems able to live on it quite comfortably with a maid and a companion and a gardener. She is a frugal old lady.'

'She always was.' He spoke encouragingly. 'So that if I were to repay the ten thousand pounds out of our father's estate, Aunt Clara's income would be assured.'

'Why yes.' She clasped her hands on the folded work, looking at him in perplexity. 'But I do not think John would allow that. And—how would you live?'

'As I have lived over the past many years—by selling my pictures.' His smile deepened. 'I assure you, dissolute as I am, I do make a certain amount of income from my painting.'

She flushed, showing the shot had gone home. 'But even if you did repay the legacy,' she said slowly, 'and even if Aunt Clara were off his hands, the rent-roll of Waveney is not a large one, and the money that should have been his has gone for ever. He will never be able to make it good, and I am beginning to think the wisest course open to him when he arrives home might be to marry money.'

'Is he thinking of marrying again?'

'He has certainly mentioned it from time to time.'

'And who is the fortunate—or shall we say unfortunate—lady who is to rescue Waveney?'

'There is a very rich widow living in a lovely house in the Close in Jerningham. Her name is Mrs. Taverner, and the Bishop's wife and I think she would be an excellent wife for John. She overdresses, and she loves wearing a great deal of jewellery in the daytime, and she is a trifle vulgar—but she is so good-hearted and kind. I think she likes John too. Why, she even visited some relatives in Sydney recently so that she could be there when his flagship put in.'

'That sounds either like devotion or pursuit.'

'You must not laugh at her. I think being mistress of Waveney would mould her into quieter, more ladylike ways, and I am sure she would make John happy.'

'And what does Susanna think about it?'

'Oh, she would much rather that he married Dorothea.'

'It seems you have all been very busy finding a wife for the Admiral.' Will's voice was dry. 'Would it not be wiser to let him find one for himself?' And then, as she did not reply, 'After all, as little Susanna said this morning, money is not the most important thing in the world.'

'It is important when you are poor,' she pointed out.

'And yet I am sure you have had a great deal of pleasure in contriving to make threepence go as far as sixpence all these years. I would even like to bet that you have felt no small triumph—and with good cause

59

—when the housekeeping books have balanced at the end of each month. Have you not, Dinah?'

'I have.' She was forced to laugh. 'Though I do not know how you know. John is very like his father in some ways—he takes a pride in Waveney, and he can be arrogant at times. But I think he really loves the place.'

'And I have always hated it,' Will said. 'Oh, it is beautiful, and as it stood originally it must have been lovelier still. But the pretentious Corinthian pillars that our grandfather built, and the Greek statues all along the front parapet, and the steps up to the grand entrance have given it to my mind a quality that can never spell out the word home.'

'You are very unlike each other really, aren't you?' Her eyes were on him thoughtfully. 'Identical twins, so alike and yet so unlike.' John, like their father, loud-voiced, a trifle bombastic and sure of himself, never taking no for an answer. And his brother—well, she did not know him very well and she could not tell. 'I should say you are more like your mother?' she hazarded.

'But we are twins,' he reminded her. 'One person in two bodies. I sometimes think that there is one mind between us, and that his is the strong side of it and mine is the weak. Where he likes to lay down the law I am diffident and afraid of my opinions, where he is sure of himself I am unsure, where he takes his success for granted I am surprised if my work should be even noticed with a kindly criticism.'

She submitted him for a moment more to that intent gaze, as if she were trying to make him out, and then she got up to go, and as he opened the door for her she hesitated before holding out her hand to him. 'I beg your pardon, Mr. Farebrother,' she said then, 'for

60

calling you dissolute. I should have known—I should have had better judgement.'

'Thank you.' He took her hand—a well-shaped, capable hand it was—with a firm grasp of his. 'We are friends, then, and allies?'

'We should not be. I should expose you and John to our friends for a pair of schoolboys. But I will not do that.' The smoke-grey eyes suddenly twinkled and the firm mouth was touched with a mischievous smile. 'I give you both permission to shelter behind my petticoats! There's only one piece of advice I would give you, however, which I hope you will consider. Jobson knows about this—deception—and I think some of the other old servants should be told as well. If I were you I would have all those who have been here longest into the library tomorrow morning and I would tell them frankly what you have told Susanna and myself. I would leave it to their discretion to keep it to themselves. It is only right that they should know. Some of them have been here at Waveney in the service of the Admiral and of his father before him for most of their lives.'

'Very well. I will take your advice.'

'Thank you, Mr. Farebrother. I think you will find that they can be trusted to hold their tongues.' And she went upstairs to bed.

For a long time after she had gone he sat on in the big room, staring into the ashes of the dead fire, and he wondered if she were in love with his brother, and he thought what an excellent wife she would have made for the Admiral if only he had been allowed by law to marry her. And when he got to this stage in his thoughts he pulled himself up abruptly. 'If I don't look out,' he thought ruefully, 'I too will fall into the Waveney habit of finding a wife for the Admiral!'

After a consultation with Jobson on the following

morning he had some of the old servants into the library as Dinah had suggested. There was the housekeeper, Mrs. Beswick, Perryman the butler, Honeysett the coachman, Grumitt the head gardener, Richards the head gamekeeper, and Barley the head groom, and as they stood there, the men cap in hand, the housekeeper with her hands folded, waiting for what he wanted with them, he told them how his brother had come to him in Paris and asked him to take his place and his name temporarily in Waveney. They did not exhibit a great deal of surprise, if some appeared to be a little puzzled, and when he had finished, feeling rather like a schoolboy confessing to a misdemeanour, the housekeeper was the first to speak.

'What did I tell you, Mr. Perryman?' She looked significantly at the butler before turning to Will. 'I told him, sir, I said directly I saw you, "If I'd not been told it was the Admiral," I said, "I'd have sworn it was Mr. Will come back again." '

'Well, you were right.' He asked them for their support in keeping the matter quiet for his brother's sake. 'I feel that more people than Mrs. Beswick will guess the truth before I've finished,' he said. 'But because I do believe that the matter may be serious and possibly could endanger the Admiral's life if it were known, I must beg you to hold your tongues.'

'You may depend on all of us, Mr. Will,' Perryman said, and the others murmured assent and then they took their departure.

In the cosy sanctuary of the housekeeper's room over dinner that evening Perryman said with a shake of his head that he hoped the H'Admiral knew what he was about. 'He never could resist a lark,' he reminded her. 'He always had the ideas, Mrs. Beswick, when they was boys here together.'

'Yes, but it was Mr. Will who was left to carry them

62

out,' the housekeeper said. 'And he got into trouble more than once over it. I only hope this little lark won't go the same way, Mr. Perryman, that I do. I was always fond of Mr. Will in the old days, and he hasn't changed, not a bit. He has that same gentle way of talking and the same quiet manner.'

They discussed it together for a time, but Honeysett discussed it with nobody. Like Grumitt, he was a man of few words, and he felt that what the Admiral and his brother did was nothing to do with him: they knew their own business best. As for Grumitt, he was pleased to think that Mr. Will was home in time to taste some of his best young vegetables, which he was sure were never grown in France. Richards, being a taciturn man, dismissed the whole thing as gentry's skylarking, and was ashamed to think the Admiral to be capable of such things, while Barley felt it was a pity they could not run a sweepstake in the servants' hall on how soon the brothers would be found out. Gentry and 'osses, he remarked philosophically to Honeysett, there wasn't much to chose between them. They could do some unexpected things between them, and the better bred they was, the queerer was the things they'd get up to.

7

Every morning after breakfast Mrs. Beswick would come to Dinah's little sitting-room to discuss the day's meals and any problems of the household. Once a month she would bring the tradesmen's books with her to be gone through meticulously with Miss Woodcock, and she would receive from her the month's wages due to the maid-servants at the Manor. But as Mrs. Beswick had already made up her mind about the meals she intended to serve and also the way in which she was going to solve her problems—such as the laziness of an under-housemaid, and the crimes of the fourteen-year-old kitchen maid who could not be got up in the mornings —Dinah only had to listen. It was in fact an interview that was quite unnecessary, though neither of the two ladies concerned would have admitted it.

After her talk with Will, Dinah had been turning things over in her mind, and the next morning, after Mrs. Beswick had left the library and come upstairs to her room, she asked her what she thought about the situation.

'Well, of course, it's not for me to say, miss.' Mrs. Beswick always began like that when she had a great deal to say. 'I must say you could have knocked me down with a feather when I heard what the Admiral and Mr. Will were about. I only hope as it don't come back on poor Mr. Will, like it's done before, when they was boys.'

'You have been at Waveney a long time, haven't you, Mrs. Beswick?'

'Yes, miss. I came to the Manor as under-housemaid thirty-five years ago. The Admiral and Mr. Will was ten years old when I first came and as like as two peas.'

'But I suppose you could tell them apart?'

'Oh I could, miss. Directly they spoke, that is to say. Mr. John was the boisterous one, Mr. Will always quieter. Mr. John would always shout at a body as if she was deaf, but Mr. Will had a gentle voice—the same as he's got now. That was why I thought it was him when he first stepped up to me in the hall. "That's Mr. Will," I thought. "And yet it can't be, otherwise I'd have been told." Because of getting the room ready you see, miss. I wonder he didn't have something to say about it this time, though. They are grown men now, not children. But he's acting just as he did when they was children: where Mr. John led, Mr. Will would follow. They were devoted to each other.'

'But when the Admiral went to sea Mr. Will did not follow him then?'

'No. That was the one thing he would not do. They was sixteen about that time, I suppose, and Sir Roger wanted both of them to go to sea, but Mr. Will wanted to paint and the rough life of the Navy was not for him. As I said, he was a quiet, gentle boy, quite unlike his brother. Sir Roger was furious. Took him away from school he did, and said he could work on the estate under his agent, and at first Mr. Will was miserable. The agent wasn't like Mr. Homer: he was a hard domineering sort of a man and was always at Mr. Will, knowing he was in his father's black books, as you might say. Then Mr. Will had this idea of riding out on his horse with a saddle-bag full of paints and canvases and he would go round the villages near and far and paint inn signs for a night's lodging, because, of course,

Sir Roger would not give him any money. And then sometimes Mr. Will would paint portraits of farmers' wives in their best dresses for to hang in their parlours, and their husbands would pay well for them too. So he managed on his own, but I don't know if he would ever have done any good if Mrs. Duncombe hadn't come to stay. He'd made himself a studio up in the old nursery and she found a stack of his pictures there and she was so struck with them that she said she would pay for him to study painting in London. She never had any children of her own and she was a very rich lady in those days—her husband was something grand up in London.'

'Did she pay for Mr. Will to go to Paris and Italy as well?'

'I really could not say, miss.' Mrs. Beswick drew herself up, slightly affronted. Nobody should ever say that she allowed herself to be questioned about her employer's private concerns, and while she might flow on happily if she were not interrupted she did not like being interrogated. 'Will that be all, miss?'

'Yes, thank you, Mrs. Beswick.' Dinah smiled a little wryly as the housekeeper left the room. She always felt that Mrs. Beswick did not approve of her position at the Manor and regarded her a superior governess in the Admiral's household: she never failed to let her know if she overstepped those bounds as she had now.

For a time she sat idly at her desk thinking about Will Farebrother. She found her interest aroused in the man and presently she made her way upstairs to the old nursery to look once more at the pictures he had left behind.

Now that she was beginning to see the character of the man who had painted them more clearly they took on a new significance. Young as he had been when they were done they showed promise and talent: that silvery

66

green field of oats, for instance, with the single scarlet poppy growing by the gate, you could feel the wind ruffling your face as it ruffled the oats like the waves of a sea behind the poppy. And here was a farmyard with a duck pond covered with green weed: you could put your hand into that water.

She came down to find Susanna looking for her. 'Aunt Dinah,' she said, 'Uncle Will says we should have Clarkson's to do the catering for my ball.'

'Clarkson's? The confectioner's in Jerningham?'

'Yes.'

'But that is absurd, with only a fortnight to go and Gunter's estimate already in.' It had been the Bishop's wife who had advised her to engage the famous London caterers in Berkeley Square. 'They do most of the coming-of-age festivities in the country—so much better than local people, my dear!' she said. Dinah had yielded to Mrs. Somerton's superior wisdom reluctantly. She liked the Jerningham tradespeople and she would have liked to employ Clarkson's as she would have liked Dewey's, the wine merchants, to supply the wines. And now it seemed that Will Farebrother agreed with her. 'I don't see how it is possible to get it done locally at such short notice.'

'That is what I said, but Uncle Will only said "Nonsense". Rather in the way Papa would have said it,' Susanna added thoughtfully.

'Where is he? I will go and speak to him.'

'In the library.' Susanna accompanied her aunt downstairs to where Will was sitting with his head in *Blackwood's Magazine*. As they entered he got up, putting the journal down.

'Susanna has told you what I think we should do about the ball supper?' he said pleasantly.

'Yes, and I'm afraid it is impossible.' Dinah looked

67

severe, but he was beginning to learn that the severity was really worry.

'My dear, it is not impossible at all,' he said gently. 'It is a matter of common sense. Do you realise that the Mayor, Dewey, is the leading wine merchant in Jerningham and it is he who has arranged this sumptuous luncheon for us all after the opening of the park? He should be asked, surely, to provide the champagne for Susanna's coming-out ball? Unless my brother put down any wine for the occasion when she was born?'

'He never had the money for such luxuries and the only wine in the cellars here when we moved in from the Grange was a little port beside a few bottles of Napoleon brandy.'

'I thought as much. The invitations are out?'

'Oh yes. We sent them off at the beginning of May. Lady Sare helped us with the list, didn't she, Susie? We reckoned there would be three or four hundred guests.'

Her mind went back to that afternoon in early May when, appalled at the magnitude of the task in front of her, she had ordered the pony trap round and driven over to Royde Park to ask Cecily Sare's help.

Lady Sare had been at home and she was shown into her private sitting-room where she was writing some letters with her little dog Nigger on her lap. She greeted her visitor warmly: she was a very charming and gentle person, quite unlike the strong-minded Mrs. Somerton.

'You have lived so quietly at Waveney,' she said, 'that it is no wonder you are finding this ball of Susanna's to be rather alarming. But I am sure it need not be, and you will wonder afterwards why you were worried about it. It is bound to be a great success, because you are so capable.'

'But I don't do a great deal at Waveney,' Dinah said. 'Mrs. Beswick does all the planning when the Admiral is home and entertaining his men-friends. I have only presided at his table as his hostess—and sometimes I have not even done that. And now that he has left this ball of Susie's for me to arrange I do not know where to begin. I must draw up a list of guests—but apart from the thirty or so relatives and old friends who will be staying in the house, where shall I start?'

'I suppose after the Admiral's relatives the Lord Lieutenant of the county should head the list,' said Lady Sare, and suggested kindly, 'Would you like me to help you with it in the Admiral's absence? Supposing you bring Susanna over with you tomorrow and spend the day here, and we go through it together? Would you like to do that?'

Dinah accepted the invitation with gratitude and the following day had seen her and Susanna driving to Royde Park in the trap and they had spent the morning over their lists.

'I do like Lady Sare so much,' Dinah now said to Will. 'She always has time to give to other people's problems.'

Susanna did not say anything. Her mind had been on other things. That had been the day when Edward Royde had come home unexpectedly: she had been sent out into the park after luncheon to give Lady Sare's little dog a run, and as she rambled through the park on the north side of the house she saw its owner walking quickly up the ride towards her. She expected him to lift his hat to her and go on, but instead he had stopped and said something about the dog. 'You need not be afraid if Nigger puts up a rabbit or two,' he told her. 'I've warned my gamekeepers not to set snares.'

'Oh I'm sure Nigger won't go after rabbits. He is a lap dog, isn't he, not a sporting type!' She spoke with some contempt, comparing the busy little creature with her beloved old Bruce.

'I think you underrate his powers. Nigger has killed a few rats in his day.' And then, as she waited for him to go, he turned and, to her chagrin, started to walk back to the house with her. 'I hear you are to have your coming-out ball in June?'

She was surprised that he should mention so frivolous an occasion. 'Yes, but I do not suppose you will come,' she said, hoping to offend him into silence, but his expression did not alter in the least. He was a most irritating man.

'Am I not to be invited, then?' he asked mildly.

'Of course you will be invited.' She was flurried for a moment, and then went on quickly, 'But, you see, you never go to balls, do you? So one imagines that you do not like to dance.'

'I like to dance when I have a congenial partner,' he replied.

'And you have not found any—congenial partners—in Jerningham?'

He frowned. 'What makes you say that?'

'Well, I have never heard of you being at any ball in Jerningham, and if you don't go to any I can only suppose that you do not find Jerningham ladies sufficiently congenial to attract you.'

'I cannot say that I do,' he replied with deplorable frankness. 'At most balls I find myself either saddled with a heavy dull girl who can only talk of hunting and horses, which I like to discuss in the club and stables, and not in the ballroom, or else I find I have a pretty flirt who expects me to pay her compliments. As in all probability I have not met her before that evening and will certainly not meet her again if I can help it, the paying of compliments does not come easily to me. I do not like flirts,' he added severely.

'Perhaps if you indulged in the art of flirting a little yourself you might enjoy it better,' she said daringly, and he saw that she was laughing at him and she thought she caught an answering spark in his eyes before he replied, 'I am afraid I am not like some more fortunate fellows, an adept at saying what I do not mean.'

Her eyes met his mischievously. 'But then, are you an adept at saying anything, Mr. Royde?' she asked.

The light left his eyes abruptly. 'You are shortly to be launched on the world, Miss Farebrother,' he said, 'and you will come to it with high hopes and expectations, I do not doubt. I am afraid I am a dull dog, but my father was a good friend to your family in the old days, and he once said to me, "There is a very fine line between wit and rudeness. It is a test of breeding to recognise that line and to keep to it." '

She bit her lip, but she said no more until they were nearing the house when she remarked quietly: 'I like this approach to your house. It is much less pretentious than the front aspect. But it needs flowers to lighten the heaviness of it—the gaiety of flowers. But there again your father might have said so much would depend on the taste—good or bad—of its owner.' And then she saw Dinah and Lady Sare on the terrace and calling the little dog she ran off to meet them. She almost thought she heard him say 'You little baggage'—of which she was quite sure his father would not have approved—as she left him, but she could not be sure. She was very sure, however, that she detested Mr. Edward Royde more than ever.

Since that afternoon she had not seen him until the musical evening at the Palace, which he had attended with his sister. He had not spoken to her or come near her, but he had stared in a peculiarly unpleasant way when she had come out of the conservatory with Captain Sloane. She supposed that his mightiness might think she was a flirt—or that Captain Sloane was a flirt—but she really did not care a button what he thought.

71

In the meantime Dinah was discussing the catering arrangements with Will. 'It was only when I met Mrs. Somerton one afternoon at Mrs. Taverner's and she said of course we would employ London caterers that I thought perhaps we should. I wrote to Gunter's and I have their estimates if you like to see them. They seem to be very expensive.'

'But I don't suppose John expects to give a coming-out ball for Susanna without spending a certain amount on it. If you engage Clarkson's and Dewey's, however, you will have the advantage of being able to consult them on the spot without a lot of tiresome correspondence. I suggest you take the carriage into Jerningham this morning and tell Mr. Clarkson and Mr. Dewey that the Admiral would like the catering for Miss Farebrother's ball to be done by local firms, and that he would be grateful to both gentlemen if they will supply lists of food and wines suitable for supper for three hundred or so guests. You can explain the delay in approaching them before by the fact that you were waiting until the Admiral returned.'

Dinah drew a breath of relief. It was a great comfort to have this quietly confident man at her elbow to advise and help her. She wondered what had made her sister Mary hate him so much. Idle, dissolute, good-for-nothing—there had been no end to the evil qualities that poor Mary had attributed to him.

Her journey into Jerningham that morning was certainly rewarding and made her a great deal happier. Both Mr. Clarkson and Mr. Dewey came out to the Admiral's carriage to hear his requirements from Miss Woodcock and both gentlemen expressed their pleasure and sense of honour at being asked to cater for Miss Farebrother's ball. Dinah drove home with her conscience eased and was able to give Mrs. Somerton a

72

particularly gracious bow as she passed her in the High Street.

The following morning Will travelled to London to see Mr. Copthorne, and he had not been wrong when he had told his brother before parting from him in Paris that the lawyer would be shocked at the situation. He was not only shocked—he was outraged.

The lawyer's offices were situated in an old house looking out over Lincoln's Inn Fields. The plate on the railing informed passers-by that the occupiers were Samuel Copthorne and Son, Solicitors and Commissioners for Oaths, and nobody seeing Mr. Copthorne for the first time would have realised that he was the son of the Son.

He was a dried-up little man in his early fifties, with greying mutton-chop whiskers that had once been ginger in colour, and a pair of steel-rimmed spectacles on his rather sharp nose. He had a disconcerting habit of glancing up at his clients over his spectacles, as if his sight was impaired by them rather than helped.

Will had only met him once in his life, some time after his father's death, when he had been in London on business connected with some pictures he had sold and had to see the lawyer about some investments representing the last of the legacy that he had inherited from the Waveney estate.

As he set foot in the lawyer's offices now and a clerk came to ask his name he said with what he hoped was sufficient dignity, 'Kindly tell Mr. Copthorne that Mr. William Farebrother is here.'

'Yes, sir. Certainly, sir.' The young man scuttled up the stairs to the lawyer's office door and Mr. Copthorne came out on to the landing to greet him. When the door was closed behind them, however, and he had motioned Will to a leather armchair in front of his desk, he said with that sharp glance of his over his spectacles,

73

'Well, Mr. Farebrother, here is a pretty kettle of fish.'

'Or shall we not say a red herring, Mr Copthorne, to be drawn across the scent at Waveney?' Will saw that his flippancy was not considered to be amusing and he went on wryly, 'I presume you have heard from the Admiral?'

'He came to see me straight from the Admiralty, before he left for Paris.'

'And you have not heard from him since?'

'I have not.'

'But I presume that when you saw him he told you what was in his mind?'

'He did, sir.'

'And may I ask your opinion of it all?'

'My opinion of what, sir? Of being required to—connive at a gross deception?' The lawyer sounded indignant and Will sympathised with him.

'I know how you must feel about it,' he agreed. 'But could you not look on it as we do—my brother and I —in the light of a joke?'

'A *joke*, Mr. Farebrother?' This was worse than ever. 'Jokes of this kind are in very questionable taste and what is more have a habit of rebounding upon their perpetrators and landing them in the courts.'

'But neither my brother nor I propose to run contrary to the law, Mr. Copthorne. There is nothing illegal, surely, in the Admiral's brother eating the Mayor of Jerningham's luncheon instead of the Admiral himself? I am not robbing the gentleman, nor am I impersonating the Admiral without his knowledge and full approval. Naturally I shall do my best not to be exposed as an impostor before he returns.'

'That is beside the point. Sir John said he depended upon me to advise and to help you wherever I could. But advise you upon what? And how am I to help

74

you? I am already a most unwilling party to this deception.'

The lawyer sounded petulant and Will tried to soothe his ruffled feelings.

'I imagine all that he meant was in matters of business,' he said. 'It was all done in such a hurry that I had no time to discuss such things before we parted. But if any legal documents arise I cannot sign them, of course.'

'You have no power to sign them—unless Sir John gave you power of attorney.' The note in the lawyer's voice suggested that there was no limit as to what lengths his client might have gone.

'No. Neither will I forge his signature.'

'Certainly not!' Mr. Copthorne was so scandalised that Will laughed.

'Believe me, I have no intention of doing so. I have managed to discover that there are funds available to my brother's agent, Mr. Homer, to pay the work-people on the estate and the outdoor servants and so on. He says he wishes to retire, but I have asked him to continue for another month or two and he has agreed to do this, and to continue to draw what money he needs from the bank in Jerningham.'

'He has had such authority for years, ever since the Admiral engaged him as his agent after Sir Roger died.'

'I have had to take him into my confidence, of course, and I have told one or two of the older servants, and Miss Woodcock knows me for Will Farebrother. My niece recognised me almost as soon as she saw me.'

'That is scarcely surprising, and she will not be the only one. They are not all fools in Jerningham either, Mr. Farebrother.'

'I am afraid you are right.' Will went on to the reason for his visit. 'Did my brother say how he proposed to

75

communicate with me? I understood that it was to be through you.'

'Yes. He will telegraph—or write to me—directly his mission is accomplished, and you will then receive a letter from me. It will be addressed to the Admiral at Waveney, but stamped with my seal, so that you know you are to open it. Inside there will simply be the words "Mission completed" and a date—the date that he expects to start for home.'

'So that we may expect him sometime during the following week?'

'That would seem to be the case.'

'But supposing I wish to communicate with him? What then?'

'I am afraid you will not be able to do so, Mr. Farebrother. He gave me no forwarding address.' Mr. Copthorne sounded smugly triumphant.

'So that if I were to learn that an anarchist—or enemy agent shall we say—is hot on his trail, I can do nothing?'

'Except what your own ingenuity might suggest,' agreed the lawyer, and actually permitted himself a frosty smile. 'I do not think that such a contingency will arise, Mr. Farebrother. Your brother gave me no reason to anticipate such a situation.'

'No, of course not. It was just an idle thought that passed through my idle mind. I am rather given to such fancies.' And taking up his hat and gloves Will Farebrother said goodbye and went on his way.

His next call was on his bank manager, who did not conceal his pleasure at seeing him. 'It is a long time since we last saw you in London, Mr. Farebrother,' he said.

Will agreed. 'And now I only want some money,' he said pleasantly.

'Certainly, Mr. Farebrother. How much?'

'A thousand pounds will be sufficient, I think. If I need any more I will visit you again.'

'You would like it in notes of twenty or fifty?'

'Hundred-pound notes would be best I think. It will be easier to carry about with me.'

'I will see to it.' The manager hurried away and was soon back with ten crisp notes, which Will put away in his pocket book. He then talked a little while about Paris and the art exhibitions there and the summer exhibition at Burlington House in London, and took his leave.

He made his way to Sweeting's on the north-west corner of Cheapside for his lunch, giving in to an impulse to see if the salmon there was as good as it had been in the past, and whether the stout for which the restaurant had always been famed was as excellently brewed. He did not find a great deal to grumble about, although he discovered one sauce to be lacking—that of a young man's appetite.

.   .   .   .   .

That afternoon Mr. Royde travelled down on the same train, but Will hastily said he was going to travel in a smoking compartment and let him travel in a different part of the train. In the evening when Edward Royde remarked to his sister that he had seen the Admiral and he had been very cool in his greeting, avoiding travelling down with him with the excuse that he wished to smoke, Lady Sare smiled and said she was not surprised. 'I expect everyone is at the poor man,' she remarked. 'I will invite him to dinner later on, when he has got over the opening of the park and Susanna's ball. She will be out then and I can invite her too. You shall take her in to dinner, Edward.' She added

77

with a spice of mischief, 'You might find her interesting.'

'Scarcely that, I think,' he replied coldly. 'Miss Farebrother strikes me as being a young woman who suffers from not having had enough spankings as a child.'

'But when the Admiral was home he was too pleased to be with her to administer them, and when he was at sea Dinah Woodcock had to be papa and mamma both, and I daresay she spoiled her a little in consequence. She is a very tender-hearted woman. But I find Susanna intelligent and charming. She may be thoughtless at times—what young woman is not at eighteen? But she is a nice child underneath the spoiling.'

'I daresay you may be right.' Her brother did not seem inclined to pursue the subject and Lady Sare remembered that a letter with a Paris postmark had arrived for him that morning, entailing the visit to London and his bankers. Poor Edward. Those letters from Paris always upset him: she felt it was long past the time when they should have ceased.

But just before he got up to go to the library to write an answer to his Paris letter he remarked drily that he did not know that the Admiral smoked. His sister smiled ruefully.

'I wish you were not so shrewd,' she said. 'There is no hiding anything from you.'

He paused on his way to the door to put his hand on her shoulder with a gentle pressure. 'My dearest Cecily,' he said, 'the Admiral is as welcome to his secrets as you are to yours—and I, God help me, am to mine.'

8

Mr. Clarkson drew up a menu for the ball-supper that equalled any London caterer's, except perhaps that the refreshments were on a slightly more substantial scale, while Mr. Dewey in promising champagne for the toasts also proposed to provide claret-cup for the ladies and unlimited brandies and sodas for the gentlemen throughout the evening.

Fortunately it was to be in June, and the head gardener foresaw no difficulty in decorating the state drawing-room at Waveney that was to be turned into a ballroom for the occasion. Will remarked that it was the first time he had ever approved of the state-rooms at Waveney. We are benefiting for the first time from our great-grandfather's ostentation, and it will save John the expense of having a ballroom built out for the occasion.'

'I wish John were here, all the same,' Dinah said with a sigh. 'It is easy to say that we are to arrange this ball for Susie, but with all these Governor's balls that he has attended on his voyages it will be dreadful if Susie's were to fall short of them. He would never forgive me.'

'I think you are as able to contrive such matters as any Governor's lady,' Will said smiling. 'And now that the catering is settled there is another even more important matter to be discussed—the question of what you and Susanna are to wear.'

Dinah stared. 'That is a thing that I have never discussed with John,' she said with dignity.

'Which is why, I suppose, Susanna has dresses that might belong to your Miss Trot, and your own are such that Mrs. Beswick would be ashamed to wear. I am sorry, Dinah,' as she flushed angrily, 'I know this is unpardonable of me, and I also know how much you have economised so that John could pay off his mortgage on Waveney, but it will not do—not for Susanna's ball with half the county here to observe and to criticise. Susanna's dress must be of white satin, and yours—' and here he paused, looking at her with a critical eye, 'yours must be in French blue taffeta silk. No other blue will do. I would like Worth to make your dresses but there will not be time. You must drive over to see Lady Sare again and find out the name of her dressmaker.'

'But she has a Court dressmaker in London—I could not—it would be the height of bad manners to impose so much—'

'Nonsense, woman!' He raised his voice and there was a tone in it now very like his brother's. 'London caterers are one thing but London dressmakers are another. Go over and see Lady Sare this morning and get that address, and tomorrow you and I and Susanna will take the early train to London and see Madame the dressmaker. It is an order!' That won a faint smile from her and he went over to her and took her hand. 'I know I am not John,' he said gently, 'but can you not look on me as somebody in whom you can trust in his absence? It is because I am an artist and have just come from Paris that I know about things like ladies' dresses, where John would know nothing about them. I will make sketches tonight of the dresses I would like to see you both wear and if she is wise Lady Sare's dressmaker will see that they are made and ready in time. I believe she will. Dressmakers are usually excellent business women.'

She wondered how he knew so much about ladies'

dressmakers and then she thought that perhaps he had painted portraits of rich men's wives in Paris and they had worn their best dresses for him just as those farmers' wives had done years ago. So once more she went to see Lady Sare and again her friend was helpful and kind and not only gave her the name and address of the Court dressmaker she employed but also wrote a letter to the lady, asking her to do her best for her friends.

On the following morning Will accompanied Dinah and her niece to London and waited in a small room downstairs examining fashion plates while upstairs they were measured and linings fitted on them to save time. While they were getting dressed again, Madame herself came downstairs to interview Mr. Farebrother.

'These are Parisian fashions, sir,' she said, holding out the sketches he had brought with him.

'Yes. The bustle over there has almost gone out: the material is flounced and bunched a little at the back with a slight draping in front. It is a prettier and more graceful fashion now.' He saw her look of puzzlement and added, 'I am Mr. William Farebrother, the Admiral's brother. I live in Paris and being in London on a visit and hearing that my niece and Miss Woodcock were planning to visit you I took the liberty of designing their dresses. I am an artist,' he explained.

'But of course! You are this great new artist that everyone is talking about in London: all my ladies rave about your pictures, Mr. Farebrother.'

'Ladies will rave about anything as long as they imagine it to be fashionable, Madame.' He dismissed the subject hurriedly. 'The important thing is, can you obtain the materials for these dresses?'

'Certainly.'

'You are happy about the designs?'

'I agree with you about the bustle, but I think Miss

81

Woodcock's bodice could be cut to show more of her shoulders and arms which are very beautiful, and I think Miss Farebrother's should be cut more simply, to show less, as she is immature as yet and inclined to be thin.'

'She is all quicksilver and gives herself no time to gather flesh on her bones. Very well. We will leave it in your good hands, and when they are finished I should be obliged if you will send the account to me—in the care of my bank. It will be forwarded to me and I will have great pleasure in settling it. It will be my present to my niece and to Miss Woodcock.' And then the ladies joined them and he said no more.

They went and sat on chairs in Rotten Row for a time, watching the élite of London riding there: a few of the riders stopped to speak to Will, taking him for the Admiral and complimenting him on his beautiful daughter. When he thought they had sat there long enough he took his companions to the Hôtel Métropole, one of the largest of the grand hotels in Northumberland Avenue, where he gave them lunch. It was a pleasant day out, marred by nothing, not even by the news when they returned home that the Mayor was calling upon the Admiral the following morning to discuss with him the arrangements for the opening day of the park, due to be held on the following Saturday.

A day or two later Lady Sare received a letter from her dressmaker thanking her for sending her the new customers and adding that she had been most interested to meet the Admiral's brother who said he was in England on a visit and had accompanied the ladies. 'He has made some beautiful sketches for their gowns,' she added. 'He must be a very clever artist. If he were not so famous I would dearly like him to design others for me.'

Lady Sare read the letter through thoughtfully, but

she did not reveal its contents to anybody, not even to her brother, and presently she tore it up and put the pieces into the grate, tucking them down into the logs with the poker so that they should be burned that evening when the fire in her sitting-room was lighted.

The Mayor's visit proved to be much less alarming than anticipated. A somewhat fussy little man, with hair plastered down and parted in the middle and with a waxed moustache, he looked what he was—a prosperous wine merchant. He drove out in his gig, arrayed in his best suit and a brown bowler hat and bright yellow boots with white uppers, and he was delighted with the reception he was given. The Admiral, he told his wife later, read the programme through and approved of it in every detail, and the little man added that now Sir John was home for good he hoped the firm of Dewey and Son would receive many more orders for wine from Waveney Manor.

Far more alarming to Will was the visit of Mrs. Taverner that same afternoon, and directly Susanna told him that her carriage was coming across the park, he ignominiously fled, leaving Dinah to bear the brunt of the visit, in what he felt to be a most cowardly fashion, although as Mrs. Taverner was the one person in Jerningham who had seen the Admiral only six months ago Dinah too felt he might be wise to make himself scarce.

The lady had had a slight argument with a friend who was staying with her before setting out. Miss Grant, who was an old enough friend to take liberties, had suggested that Mrs. Taverner should wait for the Admiral to call upon her.

'He knows where you live,' she pointed out. 'If I were you I would not lay myself open to a charge of running after the poor man directly he sets foot in Waveney.'

83

'The Admiral has been home over a week now,' said Mrs. Taverner. 'No doubt his time has been fully occupied and I do not mean to stay long. I thought I would ask him to dinner here after the opening of the park next Saturday. Nobody can take exception to that, surely?'

'I should have thought another day would have been better,' said Miss Grant. 'Remember he will have had to eat the Mayor's luncheon, and I hear they are starting with turtle soup, which seems an unfortunate choice for June.'

'Gentlemen never mind what they eat,' said Mrs. Taverner comfortably, 'as long as there are plenty of wines to go with it. And there should be some good claret at all costs; Dewey's have always been noted for their clarets.' She gave an exclamation of annoyance. 'There! A button has burst off my glove. Ring the bell, dear, if you please. Hortense must fetch me another pair.'

As they waited for the French maid—it was a fad of Mrs. Taverner's that her lady's maid should be French —to fetch the gloves Miss Grant remarked that she thought a larger size would be better. 'I noticed how tight they were when you were getting them on,' she added, and then glancing down at her friend's feet asked if she thought the high-heeled shoes she was wearing would be suitable for a warm day. 'If you wore half a size larger you would be able to play croquet at your party next week.'

'I do not wish to play croquet,' Mrs. Taverner said in a plaintive voice. 'I like to allow other people to rush about and get hot. I prefer to sit under the trees and talk.'

'Hum!' said Miss Grant.

'I don't know why you say that, dear,' said her friend. 'The shoes I am wearing may pinch a little—I do not say they do not. But large feet are so inelegant.'

They set out for Waveney amicably enough, however, because they were great friends, although Miss Grant was slightly triumphant when they found that the Admiral was not at home. Miss Woodcock received the ladies alone in the big drawing-room, and Mrs. Taverner noticed with some disapproval that she was wearing a purple serge dress that had seen better days, and as they drove home she remarked on the fact to her friend.

'I saw that dress before I left for Australia,' she said. 'She has worn it constantly over the past two and a half years. I think she might have put on a newer and prettier dress, knowing, as she must, that now the Admiral is home they may expect a stream of callers at Waveney.'

'Perhaps Miss Woodcock does not possess any newer or prettier dresses,' suggested Miss Grant.

'She has no taste,' said Mrs. Taverner. If she had known that the 'Admiral' and Susanna spent most of their afternoons hiding from callers she would have been more annoyed still.

There was no escaping the lady's garden-party at her house in the Close on the following week, however. She had impressed on Dinah that she would expect them all. 'It is not to be anything grand,' she said. 'We are having lawn tennis for the younger people, and croquet as well, although I remember that the Admiral played both games as vigorously as any boy in Sydney.'

'Can you play lawn tennis?' asked Susanna later that evening, as Dinah scolded them both mildly for having run away and left her to the mercies of Mrs. Taverner.

'I cannot,' said Will. 'Neither can I play croquet, or bowls or cricket or any other game that Mrs. Taverner may see fit for her guests to indulge in.'

85

'But what excuse can you make?' asked Dinah apprehensively. 'For not playing lawn tennis or croquet I mean?'

'He has strained a muscle in his arm,' Susanna said swiftly. 'It is much better, but the doctor says he must not put any strain on it.'

'Susanna, you are a marvel,' her uncle said admiringly. 'That would not have occurred to me in a week.'

'Susie is *not* a marvel and she is very wrong to encourage her uncle to tell lies,' said Dinah severely, and as her eyes met Will's he laughed.

'Don't be a sourpuss,' he pleaded. 'I like you so much better when you laugh.'

Reluctantly then she did laugh. 'But you will find it no laughing matter sitting under the trees in that garden and chatting to Mrs. Taverner about Sydney. I would advise you to go down and see Captain Ashworth tomorrow morning: he has plenty of books about Australia that you might do well to borrow. And what about your speech for the opening of the Farebrother Park?'

'That is nothing,' he said carelessly. 'I shall just say how honoured we are as a family, and what pleasure it has been to us to give the park to the people of Jerningham and that I hope they will all spend many happy hours there. And then Susanna will pull the cord and the statue will be revealed to the admiring crowd, and all will be over.'

'And what about your speech after the luncheon?' she asked. 'You will be expected to respond to toasts, don't forget.'

'By that time if I have had enough wine I shall be able to speak beautifully on anything and everything that comes into my head, and if I am lucky my audience will also have had so much to eat and drink that they

86

will be too torpid to understand a word. Which will be just as well,' he added more soberly.

'I wish you would not treat it all as such a joke,' Dinah said crossly.

'But it is a joke,' he reminded her. 'And not my joke, but dear old John's.' To himself he added, 'And a damned stupid one too.' It was the nearest he got in his thoughts to censuring his brother.

9

It was a glorious day for the opening of the Farebrother Park: no tearing wind or pouring rain was
there to drown Will's speech or to spoil Susanna's unveiling of her father's statue. Everyone was there for
the occasion, the Bishop and his family, the Lord Lieutenant of the county and the local Member of Parliament, with their wives, and with Susanna at his elbow
Will made few mistakes.

Lady Sare he recognised by seeing Mr. Royde with
her, but he liked best the people who came up to him
saying, 'You do not know me, Sir John, but I have
watched your career with interest,' or 'I am a relative
of the Bishop's and though we have never met before,'
and so on. It made him happier to greet these strangers
than those for whom Susanna, with her hand on his
arm, prepared him with a sudden pull on his coat sleeve
and a cry of, 'Oh, here is Lord So-and-so,' or, 'There
is Lady Such-and-such,' or 'Mrs. Taverner and Miss
Dudley, how nice to see you here,' warning him that he
knew them very well.

Luncheon at the Town Hall was fully as heavy and
indigestible as such luncheons usually are, and as the
leading Councillors were all there at the top table with
their wives, he got on fairly well, even though Susanna
was separated from him by the Mayor. But when he got
up to speak he managed to go back to the days when he
was a schoolboy at Waveney, avoiding any reference

to a nautical career, and as he dwelt on the pranks that he and his twin brother got up to in the town his speech brought laughter and clapping and stamping of feet.

'Uncle Will,' Susanna remarked to Dinah later, 'is a much better speaker than Papa. He makes people laugh, while Papa makes them yawn.'

'How do you know?' asked her aunt. 'You have never been to a public luncheon before.'

'That is why I noticed it,' Susanna said. 'The Mayor turned to me and said how glad he was that we had the Admiral back again for good: he had never heard him make a better speech.'

'I am not happy about the Ashworths,' said her aunt. 'I noticed when your uncle was apologising to Mrs. Taverner for not being able to play tennis at her party next week—because of his "strained muscle"—the Captain exchanged glances with Dorothea and they both smiled. I think they smell a rat.'

'They haven't been near us since Uncle Will has been here, have they?' agreed Susanna. 'It is unlike them. Usually when Papa is home they are in almost every day.'

There was something else worrying Dinah and when she was alone with her niece she said reproachfully, 'I noticed that Edward Royde came up to speak to you, Susie, and you turned your back on him. I know you don't like him, dear, but a lady is never rude.'

'I suppose that is a gentleman's prerogative,' said Susanna resentfully. 'The last time I spoke to Mr. Royde he lectured me and I haven't forgotten it.'

'What did he lecture you about?'

'I don't know.' Susanna moved impatiently. 'Aunt Dinah, don't scold. He was only being pompous and stuffy, as he usually is.'

'You tell me not to scold, Susie, but I must if I see you doing anything that will hurt our friends and yourself. I want you to be a gentlewoman with gentle manners, not a hoyden with no manners at all. Lady Sare is our friend and the next time you meet her brother I hope you will remember that and afford him at least common politeness.'

Dinah did not often find fault with her niece and the severity of her rebuke went home. Susanna went over to her and kissed her. 'I'm sorry,' she said penitently. 'Very well, Aunt Di. I will try and be polite to Lady Sare's odious brother.'

The following morning after church Will walked round to the Grange and asked Captain Ashworth if he could borrow some books on Australia. 'Dinah tells me you have some,' he added.

'Of course. I shall be delighted.' The Captain took him into a room where there was a case full of books. 'I am afraid it is the full extent of my library,' he said. 'I am not a reading man, preferring a game of chess.'

'Yes,' said Dorothea from the doorway, and she laughed. 'When are you coming to give Papa that game, Mr. Farebrother? It can be played with the left hand, you know.'

He looked from one to the other quickly and saw the laughter in their faces and smiled ruefully. 'So you have guessed?' he said.

'Not entirely.' The Captain made him sit down and sent a servant for sherry for their guest. 'I'll admit I was puzzled from the start—I wondered in fact if you and John had played another of your old tricks on the inhabitants of Jerningham, and then a few days later I received a letter posted from Marseilles. It was in code —a code that John and I invented when we were midshipmen together. It was not signed but it told me that he had gone on a mission and that you were taking his place in Waveney and asking me to be kind to you. That is why we have avoided Waveney since you have been there: we were afraid that some inadvertent word might betray you to the servants.'

'Most of them know already. Dinah thought it best that I should tell them and trust to their loyalty and affection to keep it dark.'

'I daresay she was right.' The Captain poured out some sherry for him. 'I presume that you want the Australian books in order to read up something about Sydney before Mrs. Taverner's party?'

'That is correct.' Will shook his head. 'I am afraid I shall not pull the wool over her eyes though.'

'Do not be too certain of that. The Admiral is home again at Waveney, and therefore everybody expects to meet the Admiral. Mrs. Taverner tells her friends that the Admiral is coming to her party, and the Admiral is there. It is perfectly simple.'

Will said he hoped it would be simple, but he sounded doubtful.

'How long does John expect to be away?' asked the Captain.

'A fortnight.'

'And you have no idea what this mysterious mission is?'

'None whatever. Have you?'

'Well, it did cross my mind that he might be trying out another of these underwater craft, highly secret, of course, and extremely dangerous.'

'You think he might have volunteered to go down in one?'

'Exactly.'

'H'm. A submersible boat—it sounds a crazy sort of craft to me.' Will turned it over in his mind. 'What, for instance, do they do with the funnels?'

'They are stowed and covered with watertight scuttles fitted over the aperture. Under water the fires are extinguished and the steam is superheated to provide motive power.'

'And how do they get them down to the right depth?'

'Partly by admitting water, and partly by means of a couple of screws in the hull which pull her down to where they want to go.'

'You said just now it was extremely dangerous. Is this because there is a risk of explosion?'

'Oh no.' The Captain smiled wryly. 'The difficulty is to get the boat up again, once she has reached the sea-bed.'

'I see.' Will's imagination shied away from the picture of John sitting there at the bottom of the sea in a boat shaped like a coffin. 'It sounds like an adventure that would appeal to my brother, but surely if he had volunteered for it there would have been no need for this—masquerade? Why did he not let me take his place openly, saying that I was here to open the park for him as he was absent on an important naval trial before finally retiring from the sea? It would have been so simple.'

'You are right, my dear fellow. Of course, there would have been no need for you to impersonate John under those circumstances. Well, I suppose we shall just have to wait until he comes home to hear what it is all about.'

'I fully expect him to be home before Susanna's ball,' Will said. 'He won't forget that.'

'Oh no, you may depend on it that he will be home for Susanna's ball.' The Captain sounded so confident that the Admiral's brother took heart. The niggling doubt that John Farebrother might not be home in time for Susanna's ball, that in fact, in the midst of the excitement and danger of this mysterious mission of his, he might have forgotten it altogether, gradually died away. This man was his brother's oldest friend and he knew him better even than he did himself. The ball was ten days away and there was plenty of time. Any day now might bring a letter saying that the mission had been completed.

.   .   .   .   .

Mrs. Taverner was a tall woman, with nut-brown hair in which nature had been lavishly helped to retain the brown by a brightness that gave it a slightly brassy look.

Her face was carefully rouged, her bones were big and therefore she did not give the appearance of being stout, and in fact she was called by some gentlemen in the county with an eye for such things a 'fine figure of a woman'.

She dressed expensively, though in colour and style her clothes were a trifle loud and her house was like herself in that it showed more wealth than taste. It was heavy with Turkey carpets and the best Kidderminster, with velvet curtains and Nottingham lace, and furniture from Maples and Waring and Gillow. The pianoforte in the drawing-room was of satinwood, there were many occasional tables of mahogany and walnut, and innumerable footstools, and a few heavy books profusely illustrated with engravings, of countries abroad —such as China and India—for the entertainment of her guests. There were no family portraits anywhere except for a large photograph of the late Mr. Taverner in Mrs. Taverner's boudoir, in which he rather resembled Mr. Dewey, and on the walls were large reproductions of the works of well-known artists, those of Landseer taking pride of place.

Mahogany-framed mirrors of vast proportions surmounted the chimney-pieces, and were flanked usually by white Parian figures of shrinking ladies, hiding their nakedness under bunches of grapes and wreaths of

93

flowers, or large bronze figures of Roman soldiers, and jugs and vases that were far too waisted to hold anything at all.

The house was spotless, looking as if its owner had just moved in, and the furniture and carpets all brand new. Outside, too, the borders in the garden were set out stiffly with bedding plants, the rose beds without a weed. Shrubs were neatly trimmed and gravel paths raked: nothing was allowed to get out of hand and no flower appeared to have any scent.

Mrs. Taverner was seated among her guests on the weedless lawn behind the house when the party from Waveney arrived, and Will found himself bowing over a tightly gloved hand.

'You shall come and sit next to me here in the shade and tell me every single thing you have done since we met in Sydney,' said Mrs. Taverner, with what he felt was meant to be a telling glance. 'Susanna, my love, I am glad to see that you have brought your tennis bat and your shoes. Captain Sloane is here and the Somerton girls, so that you will be able to have plenty of games. Ella Somerton is arranging them for me, helped by Mr. Fells.'

Mr. Fells was the youngest curate in the parish of St. Anselm's and until Captain Sloane had come to stay with Miss Dudley he had been the most sought-after young man in Jerningham.

Susanna went off happily to put on her rubber-soled shoes and joined the party of young people round the tennis net, and on being asked if he would like to play Will brought out the plea of the weak wrist and Mrs. Taverner patted the chair beside hers with the purring pleasure of a cat who has her mouse within reach.

But instead of talking about his voyage home and his delight to be with his old friends again—and one old friend in particular—her Admiral persisted in talking gravely about Australia and Sydney. Had she ever visited a sheep ranch? Very interesting places, those ranches. And the sheep farmers were more interesting still. Did she like the new houses in Sydney? Did she not think them superior in some ways to those that were being built in England? Had she heard from her relatives since she had been home? It was a pity that mail took so long in coming, but the opening of the Suez Canal had improved communications with India and Australia a great deal and no doubt would be better still when the alterations were finished. And how delightful her garden was looking: her gardener must be a prize. Going from one thing to another and talking all the time, smoothly, blandly, leaving her no time to put in a word herself, and backed up by Captain Ashworth on her other side who put in a word for steam against the old-fashioned sailing ships whenever it seemed that the "Admiral" was running out of ideas.

Mrs. Taverner was irritated, puzzled and becoming annoyed by the time tea was served under the trees, and her annoyance deepened when Mrs. Somerton bore down upon the guest of the afternoon and appropriated him in her turn.

As the determined lady took a seat beside him Will looked desperately for Dinah, but she was deep in conversation with Miss Grant and there was no help there.

'Ah, Admiral,' said Mrs. Somerton, 'so nice to see you back again and looking so well—if a trifle thinner than you were? Never mind. Waveney will soon put that right. The Bishop and I were wondering if we might bring his sister Ruth to Susanna's ball? She has been living in Paris lately and knows your brother Will very well.'

A pit was yawning in front of him, and while he murmured that it would be a pleasure and that Susanna

95

would send Miss Somerton an invitation he wondered who the devil Ruth Somerton might be. Nobody he knew very well, that was quite certain—unless she was that gushing female in the flowing serge dress and sandals, who had attached herself to him at the party in Madame Merceau's salon? A horrible woman. He pulled himself together remembering that the ball was a week away and that the Admiral should be home long before it took place. 'You were saying?' he said.

'The Bishop and I were surprised to hear from Susanna that you are employing Clarkson's to do the catering for her ball. I hope they will make a success of it.' Mrs. Somerton did not sound too sure.

'I am sure they will,' said Will enthusiastically.

'At the Palace all our large parties are catered for from London,' went on Mrs. Somerton. 'We had Gunter's in Berkeley Square for Ella's coming-out dance two years ago.'

'So Miss Woodcock told me,' smiled Will.

'Well, it is very good of you to employ local firms, of course.' Mrs. Somerton still sounded doubtful.

'Not *good* of me surely, Mrs. Somerton?' Will said genially. 'It is not only my duty to support such firms but my pleasure to do so.'

Like Mrs. Taverner, Mrs. Somerton became strangely silent after that. It occurred to her, as it had occurred to her friend, that the Admiral had sadly changed. In the old days he had never had any opinions of his own where entertaining was concerned: he left such matters to his housekeeper and to Miss Woodcock, who, being diffident and uncertain of her powers, had always come to the Bishop's wife to be told what to do. There was that occasion for instance when Waveney had entertained a Royal Duke. It was the Bishop's wife who insisted that some of the Admiral's aristocratic relations should be asked to stay in the house during the visit, and it was the Admiral's Aunt Margaret, a Countess, who eventually consented to be his hostess for the occasion. That she needed more waiting upon than the Royal Duke was neither here nor there.

Tired of being attacked by managing ladies under the trees, directly tea was finished Will left the Dean to take his place and made his way to a bench beside the tennis lawn where he watched Susanna playing with Captain Sloane against Ella Somerton and Mr. Royde. He noticed that the Captain spared no effort at being gallant to his partner, murmuring criticisms of their opponents as he handed her the balls in a way that made her eyes dance with laughter. Susanna was radiant that afternoon and it worried her uncle a little. Mr. Royde slammed balls at the Captain with a viciousness that he was quite unable to counter, but the fact that they were being heavily defeated had no effect on him and his partner at all: they seemed to have no eyes for anyone except each other.

The gentlemen then made a four, Mr. Royde and Mr. Fells against Captain Ashworth and Captain Sloane, and when that was over the ladies took possession of the lawn, Ella Somerton with Susanna for her partner against her sister and Dorothea. At this point most of Mrs. Taverner's male guests had abandoned a rather tiresome game of croquet for the tennis lawn, to applaud the ladies and act as referees. It was a long game, much drawn out, with a great deal of laughter and argument on both sides as to which balls were in and which were not, the onlookers being appealed to for their judgement with many arch glances from the Bishop's elder daughter.

Will found himself sharing his bench with Captain Sloane who took every opportunity to applaud Susanna's play, with many a loud 'Well played, Miss Farebrother!'

97

While a point was being argued on the lawn Will commented with a smile, 'Miss Ella Somerton is very like her mother, is she not? I feel sure that she has the same ability for organising fêtes and charity bazaars as she has for organising a game of tennis.'

The Captain agreed, adding that it was a pity Miss Somerton was so plain.

'Plain? Do you think so?' Will sounded surprised. 'I think she is a very nice-looking young woman. The man who marries Miss Ella will be a very lucky fellow.' He dropped his voice confidentially: 'The Bishop is a rich man and everybody knows that he intends to make handsome settlements on his two daughters when they marry. I only wish poor little Susanna could look forward to a similar fortune, but when one inherits a crippled estate there is nothing to spare. My father was a most improvident man.' He sighed and then went on more cheerfully, 'However, that is all past now and the child was promised a splendid coming-out ball and she is to have it. I hope we shall see you there?'

'I would not miss it for the world,' said the Captain. He looked rather thoughtful, however, and allowed Susanna to get a ball over the net without the fervent 'Well *played*!' Will continued blandly: 'It should be quite a brilliant affair for Waveney. The house is being stretched to the uttermost to accommodate all the members of our family who are coming for it. I did not realise we had so many, but then we never see them from one year's end to the next. They are too wealthy for us at Waveney. I wish we had more horses in the stables: I shall have to hire some for the carriages and trust they don't kick them to pieces.'

Captain Sloane did not seem to be listening. His attention had wandered away from the tennis lawn and was directed at a daisy root in the grass at his feet, as if he was wondering what on earth it was doing there

98

in Mrs. Taverner's lawn. Will thought it was time he joined Captain Ashworth.

Mrs. Somerton had asked Miss Dudley and her nephew to dinner that night, with Mr. Fells commanded to be there to talk to Miss Dudley about the bazaar that was to be held for the Zenana Mission in September, and when they were alone together afterwards the Bishop's wife said that she was glad she had thought of asking the Admiral if they might bring his sister Ruth to Susanna's ball. 'I think the Admiral would be so splendid for Ruth,' she added.

'In what way?' asked the Bishop obtusely.

'As a husband, of course, my dear. It is high time Ruth got married.'

'Past time, if you ask me,' said the Bishop unkindly. 'She is far too much of a blue-stocking, though, to attract a fellow like Sir John.'

'Don't believe it, Hector. Ruth is not exactly a blue-stocking. I know that she affects to patronise the arts—which makes her unfortunately a little patronising in her manner to anybody who is not as artistically minded as herself. Though if being artistic means dressing in that extraordinary fashion of loose hair and flowing dresses and wearing no stays, then all I can say is that I'm glad I am not artistic. But Ruth is a dear girl and I'd like to see her settled, and I think the Admiral might well be drawn to somebody out of the ordinary if you see what I mean. When she comes for the ball I shall make her stay at least a month.'

'I seem to remember that the last time she came she brought her box of paints with her,' the Bishop reminded her. 'She dropped them about on my study carpet while she was making that very unflattering portrait of me and you said you would never invite her again.'

'Oh well, one says these things at the time,' said Mrs.

99

Somerton tolerantly. 'I am very fond of Ruth, really, in spite of her funny ways.'

The Bishop had something else on his mind. 'That young chap Sloane—I know he is Miss Dudley's nephew and comes from a good family, but I did not quite like the way he was hanging round Ella tonight.'

'A lot of young men hang round Ella, my dear,' said his wife cheerfully. She had noticed with satisfaction the Captain's return of allegiance to her daughter. 'Captain Sloane is a very charming young man. He has no money, of course, but I don't think that will matter. Miss Dudley tells me that if he stays in the Army he has many important relatives who will see that he gets promotion quickly.'

'And is he going to stay in the Army, my dear?'

'I feel quite sure he will,' said Mrs. Somerton, telling herself that if the Captain became engaged to Ella his mother-in-law would see that he did stay in the Army.

'How very pretty little Susanna looked this afternoon,' said the Bishop. 'She told me she was getting very excited about her coming-out ball next week.'

Mrs. Somerton smiled pityingly. 'They are doing it on the cheap,' she said. 'The Admiral confirmed what I had heard—that he is employing local firms to do the catering. There is no money at all in that quarter, I'm afraid, but no doubt he will do his best for Susanna when the time comes. It is a pity that the child is such a flirt.'

'I have not noticed it,' said the Bishop.

'But then you never notice anything, Hector.'

'No, my love, I'm afraid I am not very perspicacious. But I find Mrs. Taverner's parties very exhausting and if you don't mind I shall go off to bed.'

·   ·   ·   ·   ·

100

Mrs. Taverner had something to say about the Admiral to her friend Miss Grant that evening. 'He was so unlike himself,' she complained. 'He did not show up to advantage at all. One missed his heartiness and—yes, his *gallantry*! He seems to have lost the zest for life that was his great attraction.'

'He may be regretting his retirement?' suggested Miss Grant.

'He was certainly more low-spirited than I have ever seen him,' Mrs. Taverner agreed.

'Give him time,' said Miss Grant, and Mrs. Taverner said she would give the dear man all the time he needed.

10

In the meantime at the Manor that evening Susanna had been in a temper from the moment they had arrived home, and she was in a temper still after they finished dinner. She refused to stay in the drawing-room and went out into the garden to sulk in the twilight.

'What on earth is the matter with the child?' Dinah wondered. 'Is she tired, do you think, after playing all those games of tennis?'

'She is as strong as a young pony,' Will said. He got up. 'I'll see if I can find out what is troubling her.' He strolled after his niece and found her in the rose garden, where a scent of honeysuckle mingled with that of old-fashioned roses.

'There is nothing like Waveney at this time of year,' he remarked. Susanna turned her back on him and examined a rose carefully, but he noticed that her fingers were trembling. 'I always forget what it is like when I am away from it,' he went on, 'but when I come back it enfolds me in its embrace as if I had never left it. Dear forgiving Waveney.'

She whirled round on him. 'I believe you did it,' she said. 'You were talking to him while we were playing that last game. You said something to him.'

'Now what did I say?' he asked soothingly. 'And to whom?'

'I wish you had never come here,' she said. 'You said something to Frank—to Captain Sloane—and afterwards he never took any notice of me at all. He helped the Somerton girls to change their horrid shoes and he carried the shoes and their bats to the carriage for them, and he left that—odious Mr. Royde to wait on me. Not that I would allow him to help me, of course. I told him I could well manage for myself and he stalked off.' She was on the verge of tears.

'My dearest child,' he began.

'I am not your dearest child!' cried Susanna, choking.

'Well, then, my beloved niece. Is that better?'

'No, it isn't, because I know you are going to say something nasty.'

'Not nasty. Unpalatable perhaps. But I hope sensible.'

'You can be as sensible as you like,' said Susanna defiantly. 'You are not going to stop me loving him. I shall marry Captain Sloane in spite of your—interference. I could see that he wasn't happy to dance attendance on Ella and Maud. What did you say to him?'

'As far as I can remember we were talking about your ball. I asked him if he was coming to it and he said he was looking forward to it very much. And then I think I told him that we expected a great number of relatives to stay and that sort of thing. The small talk that passes for conversation at such parties as Mrs. Taverner's.'

The anger cleared from her face. She slipped her hand into his arm. 'I'm sorry I was rude,' she said. 'But now that you know him better you do like Captain Sloane, don't you?'

'No. I cannot say that I do.'

The hand left his arm abruptly. 'But of course you don't know him at all!'

'I daresay you are right, my dear.'

'Oh, how I wish you would not agree with everything I say!'

'I do not agree with everything you say, but it is not polite to contradict a lady.'

'There are moments, Uncle Will, when I hate you!'

'I'm sorry for that. What can I do to make you love me again?'

'Stop treating me like a child for one thing.' She sounded petulant. 'I suppose Aunt Dinah has been talking to you and you both think Mr. Royde would make the perfect husband?'

'If your aunt thinks that she may be almost right, except that I would say scarcely any husband is perfect —he would be a monster if he were. I would say however from the little I have seen of him that Mr. Royde would make any girl a very excellent husband—if he happened to care for her. But I could not see anything in his manner this afternoon that made me think he was the least interested in you, my love, so that you have nothing to fear in that quarter.'

'Oh.' She was a trifle nonplussed and then she went on, defending her opinion of Mr. Royde, 'Ella Somerton thinks he's awful.'

'She is put out of course because he is not interested in her either. Mr. Royde has much to offer any girl however and I should say that the Bishop's elder daughter would give her eyes if he appeared at the Palace in the light of a suitor.'

'Do you think so?' Her hand came back again into his arm. 'I hate Edward Royde,' she said then decidedly.

'I feel for him. It is not nice to be hated.'

'I don't really hate you though. But you must admit that you can be very aggravating at times.'

He covered the caressing little hand with his. 'I am only acting as your papa might act, my love,' he said gently. 'When he comes home maybe he will like Captain Sloane desperately and detest Mr. Royde.'

'Oh no, he will never do that. He and Mr. Royde get on together like a house on fire.'

Will was very glad to hear it. 'The dew is falling,' he said. 'Your slippers will be wet. Come back into the drawing-room and sing us one of your pretty songs before you go to bed.'

She came back and naughtily sang 'I attempt from Love's fever to fly in vain', which was not quite what he had meant. Something soothing about roses and June and moon was what had been in his mind and he was sure that she knew it because she stooped over his chair to kiss him good night with a wicked look in her eyes before she went upstairs to bed.

'You have calmed her down,' Dinah said when they were alone.

'Yes. Poor little Susanna. She was only suffering from an attack of jealousy because Captain Sloane had the bad taste to single out the Bishop's elder daughter for his attention during the last part of the afternoon. It was, after all, Miss Somerton's turn: he had devoted himself to Susanna for the greater part of the time.'

'I do not like that young man,' Dinah said.

'Neither do I. I feel that should Susanna marry him he might spend most of his leisure hours calculating just how many years my brother has to live.'

'Don't!' She shivered. 'I hope it will be a long time before Susie inherits Waveney and I am sure she does too.' She paused. 'I wish she did not dislike Mr. Royde so much.'

'He is at least ten years older than she is, my dear.'

'She probably finds him dull as well, but there are many worse faults than dullness.' She hesitated and then continued: 'It is because I am dull that I have been allowed to look after John and his daughter and his home ever since Mary died. If I had been fashionable and a beauty or even a wit I could not have stayed on

105

a day after the funeral. But—a man may not marry his dead wife's sister—and it was not considered possible for the Admiral to be attracted to me in any other way. I have always been a dowd and I am plain enough to stir nobody's jealousy or interest. If gossip arose—as sometimes it did—Lady Sare was my friend and saw to it that it died quickly. And so I stayed.' Lectured by John when he was home, and lectured by his servants when he was at sea: Will could see it all and he admired the courage of this pale dull woman immensely. He had remembered her at his brother's wedding as a tall dark-haired girl with critical grey eyes and a cool smile. That smile had become painfully diffident, the grey eyes sadly apologetic for short-comings, and he was angry with somebody for having caused that change though he did not know who it was.

'Was that why you fought so hard against the blue dress for Susanna's ball?' he asked.

'Yes.' She looked unhappy. 'I still feel that a black one would have been more suitable.'

He ran his eyes over her critically. 'I assure you that a black dress as I would have liked to see it cut on you would not have been at all suitable,' he said drily, and saw her colour up before she laughed.

'You are trying to make me blush,' she said. 'It is all the years you have spent in France, I suppose.'

'They are a depraved lot over there,' he agreed, and the twinkle in his eye made her laugh again. As she got up to leave him he took the hand she held out to him in both of his and for a moment she thought he was going to kiss it in the French fashion, but instead he let it drop and only said gently: 'I am glad I came back to Waveney. I did not want to come—it holds very bitter memories for me. But the thought of little Susanna—and of you—will do much to soften those other

106

memories when I am back in Paris. I shall think of Waveney more kindly in future.'

As he went to John's bedroom that night he thought to himself, 'Twelve days gone. Only two more and then we should have heard from him. Or he may be home.' Somehow the thought of his brother's return was not quite as welcome as it had been. He found that he would not object to passing a few extra days in Waveney in the company of a calm and kindly woman. Dinah Woodcock brought an unaccustomed serenity to his restless spirit.

The next few days passed quickly. The ball was now only two days away and already the caterers were in and out of the house, bringing trestle tables to be stacked in the studio coach-house until they were wanted, while the head gardener was consulted about flowers on the tables and in the ballroom, and the housekeeper enquired about tablecloths. The house was filled with people, bustling, hurrying, giving orders and taking them. Old servants were pressed into service from the village to scrub and polish, housemaids flew in and out of bedrooms doing last-minute bed-making, brushing up hearths, polishing mirrors and tables, while Perryman and the young footman counted and polished silver and took shining breakfast trays from their baize covers, the old man grumbling because there was not more help.

'Economising is all very well,' he told his young helper grimly, 'but there's limits to what a man can do. In the old days, when Sir Roger was alive, there was three footmen besides bootboys galore. Now there's only you and me and that young limb of a Percy who is no good to anybody. He can't even be trusted to fill the lamps.' He grumbled on as he polished, thinking back to the heyday of Waveney when money had been spent like water. 'It's all wrong for a woman to be left in charge when the master of the 'ouse is away,' he went on. 'That Miss Woodcock now, she's no manner of use in looking after a 'ouse this size. What did she come from after all? A small country 'ouse what was 'alf a rectory as far as I can make out, and she tries to run Waveney like as if it was a rectory too, cheese-paring something 'orrible. Mrs. Beswick don't like 'er and never 'as. She says she 'obnobs.'

'Hobnobs?' The young footman took a soft brush to brush up the crest on the bulging sides of a large coffee-pot. 'What's she mean by that, Mr. Perryman? Mrs. Beswick, I mean.'

'Well, one morning last winter Miss Woodcock comes into that little sitting-room of hers and sees one of the 'ousemaids—a new girl she was, a flighty piece too—doing of the fireplace and blubbering because 'er 'ands was bleeding. So what does Miss Woodcock do but ask what was the matter, and of course they was only broken chilblains which all of the 'ousemaids suffer from winter-time. And Miss Woodcock must go and wash 'em off 'erself, and she tears a piece off of one of the H'Admiral's old shirts what had been put out for the Jerningham Ladies' Sewing Circle for to make into aprons for the old women in the St. Anselm's alms-'ouses, and she binds up the girl's 'ands and gives her a new pair of gloves to wear for doing of the grates, the old 'uns being full of 'oles.'

'Well, that was kind of her,' commented the young footman, mystified as to where Miss Woodcock had erred. 'Why was Mrs. Beswick so angry?'

'As Mrs. Beswick said,' Perryman told him with dignity, 'a lady would have done no such thing. She would have told the girl to go straight to the 'ousekeeper and ask 'er to see to 'er 'ands for 'er. She would never have done it 'erself. That was Mrs. Beswick's place.'

'I see,' said the footman.

'And don't rub too 'ard with that brush,' went on Perryman severely, 'or you'll scratch the silver. Use the leather.'

In the meantime Mrs. Beswick was hard put to it to find extra rooms for the servants that their guests would bring with them. The Countess would have her own maid, an acid lady by the name of Miss Tillot, held in quite as much awe by the housekeeper as her mistress the Countess. 'Do you think Miss Tillot would mind sleeping in the old nursery?' she asked Dinah doubtfully. 'It needs cleaning and fresh curtains put up, and there are some of them pictures stored there that Mr. Will left behind.'

'Those can be moved down to my sitting-room for the time being,' Dinah said. 'They will come to no harm there. And the old nursery is a beautifully airy room. I should have thought two or three of the ladies' maids could have slept there.'

Mrs. Beswick said she did not think Miss Tillot would like that. 'But I could put three of the other maids there,' she added, 'and Miss Tillot could have the little dressing-room on the far side of her ladyship's sitting-room. Then she would be handy if her ladyship wanted anything at night.'

Dinah said that was a splendid idea and happening to see Will on his way through the hall she told him that she had promised to take care of his pictures.

'I'd forgotten there were any up there,' he said, and added, 'When all this is over and the guests departed can I depend on you to see that they are packed up and sent to me in Paris?'

She said she would be pleased to do so and went on into the morning-room to her lists of acceptances and last-minute requests to be met in Jerningham, though the little station at Waveney had been opened again especially for the occasion. And staring at those lists,

109

pencil in hand, it suddenly occurred to her what a very bleak place Waveney would be when the Admiral's brother had gone.

'This is absurd,' she scolded herself. She pushed the lists aside and went over to the mirror above the chimney-piece, taking stock of the few grey hairs in the dark ones, of the fine lines round her mouth and eyes. 'To fall in love—at my age. It is ridiculous—absurd. And with such a man as Will, "foot-loose and fancy-free".' She made a sad little face at her reflection and went back to add to her lists a further one of the rooms that would need vases of fresh flowers in them on the morrow when the guests arrived.

11

On the evening of the twelfth of June, after the household had retired for the night, a stranger called to see the Admiral.

Perryman, longing to get to his bed, went to ask Will if he would see him. 'It's very late, sir,' he complained. 'And he looks like one of them Eyetalians Mr. Scareycheney brought with him.'

Will told him to show the man into the library where he was indulging in a night-cap before going to bed himself, and as the man came into the room he saw what Perryman meant. His visitor was small and blackhaired, with black eyes that glittered with excitement: he also had two front teeth missing that might have been due to an excitable Latin temperament.

'What can I do for you?' he asked as the door closed behind the butler.

'You can give me five hundred pounds,' the stranger said in broken English, 'if you wish to save your brother's life. I know you, Mr. William Farebrother. I know you are not this Admiral Sir John. He is not in England, but we know where he is. You may be sure of that.'

'When you say "we",' Will said patiently, 'whom do you mean?'

'The Brotherhood of the Revolution,' said the little man. He tapped himself on the chest proudly. 'I am Mario Calbanisi himself.'

'I am afraid I have never heard of you or your

brotherhood,' Will said quietly. 'And if you do not wish to spend the night in the local lock-up I suggest you take yourself off to wherever you came from as quickly as you can.'

Signor Calbanisi sat down on a library chair and folded his arms defiantly. 'I not move,' he announced, 'until you give me the money.'

'Why should I give you any money?' asked Will.

'To save your brother's life. If I go without the money I telegraph to the Brotherhood in Paris and they arrange that he is assassinated.'

'You are making a mistake, I am afraid,' Will said. 'I must make allowances for you because I can see that you are slightly deranged. You are speaking to Admiral Sir John Farebrother now.'

'You think I believe that?' The little man settled himself more firmly in the chair while Will studied him thoughtfully, remembering his conversation with Mr. Copthorne and the lawyer's advice that should such a contingency as this arise he would have to depend on what his own ingenuity might suggest. He wondered what course it would be best to pursue. There was a possibility that his visitor was armed, but he could see no suspicious bulge under his coat and he decided to chance it. He got up and rang the bell and when Perryman came, looking still more injured at being kept up, he said, 'Perryman, will you please ask Jobson to come here? And then go to bed. You will have a long day tomorrow.'

'Thank you, Sir John.' The old man shuffled off and the Italian shot an uneasy glance at Will, having caught the title given him by the servant. It might have occurred to him that he had made a mistake. 'I suppose you came over to England with Mr. Scaravicini?' Will said.

'I come with him, yes, but he not pay me enough. So I leave him—in the applecart.'

112

Jobson came into the room and Will greeted him smiling. 'Ah, Jobson,' he said, 'we are faced with a little difficulty here and I would appreciate your advice. This gentleman says he is an important member of a Brotherhood of Revolution—whatever that may be. He imagines that I am an impostor and that the real Admiral Farebrother is on the Continent somewhere, waiting to be assassinated by this mysterious Brotherhood. The only way in fact to save him is for me to pay Mr. Calbanisi here the sum of five hundred pounds. I feel for our own sakes we should offer him hospitality for the next few days, but the problem is—where are we to put him? From tomorrow onwards the house will be full from attic to cellar and I would not put him in the cellar, anyway, at the risk of the wine with which it is at the moment filled. Can you think of anywhere short of the Jerningham Police Station where he can be held until we have had that letter from Mr. Copthorne?'

Jobson thought a while in silence and then he said tentatively, 'There's the gamekeeper's hut, sir.'

'Of course. That hut on the edge of Martin's Spinney about a mile from Martin's Farm. Does anybody come that way?'

'Only gamekeepers watching out for poachers in the autumn and winter. This time of year nobody goes nigh it.'

'That's the very place then. Can we find our way to it in the dark?'

'It's not quite dark, sir. There's a moon.'

'So there is. We had better place a gag in his mouth, if you can find a stout pocket-handkerchief, and at the same time perhaps you can lay your hands on a length of rope without attracting too much attention?'

'I daresay there will be some in the cupboard in my

113

room, sir. I usually keep a coil by me in case port-manteaux need cording.'

'Excellent. Be as quick as you can while I keep this gentleman with me. Oh yes,' as the Italian, not quite understanding but aware that something was being planned between the two Englishmen that might involve him in discomfort, if not in personal danger, got slowly to his feet. 'You will stay with me, signor.' Will opened a drawer in the writing-table where he was sitting and produced a pistol that he had found there in a locked drawer soon after his return to Waveney. 'It may sur-prise you to learn that I am an expert shot. I learned here when I was a boy—my father's head gamekeeper was a first-class tutor. While my servant is gone you will sit on that chair and you will not move.' He cocked the pistol and kept it trained on the man, who, perhaps understandably, did not move.

Jobson came back with the cord and the handkerchief and between them they tied his hands behind his back and put a gag in his mouth. They then marched him smartly through the French windows and once outside took him swiftly through the grounds to the park. It was about a mile and a half from there to the spinney, but although the path to the hut was overgrown they found it fairly easily.

'There used to be a padlock,' Will said. 'The key was kept under the eaves.' He felt along it. 'How kind it is of country people not to change their ways. Here it is!'

They marched Mr. Calbanisi into the hut, which was stoutly built of stone with a slate roof and very small barred windows. There was a chair there and they sat him in it and left him bound, though removing the gag. And then telling him that Jobson would be along in the morning with some food and water they shut the door on him and locked the padlock.

'I do not like blackmailers,' Will said as they walked

back to the Manor. 'And an unbalanced creature like a self-confessed revolutionary might be dangerous. We do not want that ball spoiled. You had better take one of the keepers with you tomorrow when you visit him.'

In the morning, however, to the delight of the Admiral's immediate family, the looked-for letter from Mr. Copthorne arrived. In it was enclosed a telegram received from the Admiral the day before and sent off from Paris. It simply stated 'Mission accomplished' and was signed with the date.

'If he was in Paris two days ago then he must be home tonight or tomorrow,' Susanna said. 'Oh, Uncle Will, it is the one thing I wanted—that he should be here for my ball!'

Will was delighted for her, but in the meantime there was the troublesome prisoner in the gamekeeper's hut to be dealt with. He was wondering if he should set him free or keep him locked up for another twenty-four hours to be on the safe side, when Jobson came to tell him that their bird had flown.

'I should think some poacher after rabbits heard him shouting and kicked the door down,' he said. 'The hinges were very rusty.'

Will was relieved to hear it. 'In my opinion the man was simply a blackmailer,' he said. 'He had probably heard some gossip about us and thought he had guessed right. There may be some genuine revolutionaries lying in wait for my brother, of course, but why they should do so one cannot guess—unless they had wind of this mysterious mission of his and wanted to stop it.' Revolutionaries would threaten most their opposites, and who, apart from John, could they be? Royalty perhaps —one of Her Majesty's relatives in a small German state? Or further south still on the shores of the Mediterranean? Why had an English Admiral been selected for the mission, after all, if it had nothing to do with

115

the sea? And why had he said it would not take much longer than a fortnight to accomplish unless there was a modern steam yacht waiting for him somewhere? He pulled himself up sharply: he was letting his imagination run away with him. 'Let us hope,' he told Jobson, 'it will be the last we hear of Signor Calbanisi.'

There was no time to think about their escaped prisoner, however, because from noon onwards the house began to fill up. Uncles, aunts, cousins—first, second, and second once removed—besides families of old friends from a distance, began to pour in, fetched by every vehicle that the Manor possessed from Waveney's little country station where the London trains were stopped for them.

The Countess was there first to take command as the Admiral's hostess for the ball, while Miss Tillot unpacked and complained bitterly about the small dressing-room where she was to sleep. It was dark, there was only one cupboard, and it looked on to a rookery which would no doubt keep her awake from dawn every day she was there.

At dinner that night over thirty guests sat down at the long table in the state dining-room, eating off porcelain that had been made for the Farebrother who had added the Palladian front to the house, every plate and dish bearing the family's coat-of-arms hand-painted on it. The Countess presided beautifully at the foot of the table, with Will as the Admiral at the head. Watching and listening and thankful that such an important member of the family had taken her place, because she was sure she could never have filled it herself, Dinah wore her old black evening dress, cut as the village dressmaker had cut it five years ago, and was happy to be unnoticed.

After dinner the gentlemen stayed to circulate the port and brandy while the ladies retired to the drawing-

116

room to listen to some music, and a great deal of advice from the Countess after each performance as to how she had heard the same piece played by expert performers.

When the gentlemen joined them she called Will to her at once and said that she hoped he would wear his decorations the following night.

'And what jewellery is Susanna wearing?' she wanted to know. 'I have seen her ball-dress and it is beautiful. I do not think I could have chosen a better one myself, and I have always prided myself on my good taste where clothes are concerned. I will send Tillot to do her hair tomorrow when she has finished with me. I hope you have not engaged a hairdresser from Jerningham, Miss Woodcock? Local hairdressers have no idea of fashion or style.'

Dinah said quickly that they had not engaged anybody to do Susanna's hair.

'Oh!' The Countess's eyes rested for a moment disparagingly on Dinah's hair and then she asked again what jewels her great-niece intended to wear.

'My mother's pearls,' Susanna said quickly. 'And a ring of hers. It was one Papa found among her jewels after she died—he thought it must have been given her by some admirer long ago, before she met him.' She saw that her uncle was listening and tried to give him the information he would need were he to be questioned about it. 'It is such a pretty one, isn't it, Papa? It is made of an amethyst, a diamond, an opal, a ruby and an emerald, set in a circle.'

'And it spells the word "adore",' said Will brusquely, and seeing the surprise in his niece's face went on, 'It is the sort of sentimental gewgaw that a lover would give a girl, Aunt Margaret, and she wore it because it was pretty and sentimental.' He turned to Dinah impatiently. 'Miss Woodcock, will you not arrange

117

some more music? I am sure my younger cousins are all longing to dance.'

Dinah sat down to play for the dancing, but as she did so she could not help wondering how Will could have known about Mary's pretty ring and what it had spelt. Unless he had given it to her himself. But he could not have done that, because she hated him. Dissolute, she had called him. Poor John's dissolute brother, 'footloose and fancy-free'. And certainly John had not seen the ring until after she had died and he came across it at the very bottom of her jewel casket, hidden under an amber necklace. *Adore*, she thought. But who had been the lover then who had given that ring to her sister? She wished, uneasily, that she had known.

The following day dawned without a cloud and blossomed into a perfect English summer's day. It seemed that between the dances that night it would be possible for the guests to sit and stroll on the terraces, and great Chinese lanterns and festoons of little glass fairy-lights in red and blue and white and amber were hung up in the trees, it being the under-gardeners' duties to see that the lights inside them were burning before it got dark.

By nine-thirty Will was in the ballroom, dressed in one of the Admiral's evening suits, his most important order hung round his neck on its ribbon beneath the neatly trimmed imperial. He looked distinguished and handsome, but restless: John should have arrived hours ago and he was prey to an anxiety that he had to keep to himself. What if there had been other crazy lunatics abroad, waiting for the Admiral on a quayside or at a railway station? He could only act his part and try to portray a perfect, unruffled host.

When Dinah came into the room he forgot his anxieties for a moment: her hair was dressed in a knot at the back of her head and under the curling fringe on

118

her wide forehead her grey eyes had caught some of the colour of the French blue of her dress. As he studied that dress and the lovely shoulders that rose from it, and the slender, proudly held figure that its cut revealed, he caught his breath a little. 'Now I know why you wore those dowdy dresses,' he said in a low voice so that the Countess, resplendent in purple and diamonds, should not hear. 'Had you worn anything like this after Mary died you could not have stayed at Waveney for a single night.'

She blushed and laughed and then suddenly became grave. 'Will, where is John? Why isn't he here?'

'He will come.' He spoke more confidently than he felt.

'But that telegram was sent off three days ago.'

'I expect him at any moment.' He looked past her to Susanna. 'Here is the little lady herself, and how very charming she looks.'

Susanna, trailing her white satin, with a tiny bouquet of pink roses in her gloved hands, came and stood beside them smiling. 'Do you like me?' she asked.

'You are beautiful,' her uncle told her. 'And you know it, you little minx.' And then the first arrivals were upon them and he had to take his place beside the Countess.

The first dance was due to start at ten o'clock and a few minutes before ten the Bishop and his family arrived. With them there came Captain Sloane and Miss Dudley and as he turned from greeting the Bishop Will was conscious of Susanna welcoming the Somerton girls. They were evidently excited about something, and he saw her listening to what they were saying and looking at Ella's left hand, before Captain Sloane took her programme to write his initials beside some dances. Then her uncle saw her say something to them and hurry away towards the entrance as if she were looking for somebody. At the same moment Jobson touched his sleeve urgently.

'Beg pardon, Mr. Will,' he said in a low voice. 'The Admiral is here.'

'I'll come at once.' Will left the ballroom and made his way upstairs and thought no more about Susanna. All he could say to himself was, 'Thank God he's come.' No anarchist had stopped him, no bomb had been thrown, no weapon fired. The problems of Waveney were once more its master's and not anything to do with his brother: he could hand them all over thankfully and return the way he had come.

.   .   .   .   .

All that day and indeed for most of the days before her ball Susanna had been sure of one thing: Captain Sloane would find an opportunity somewhere—maybe on the terrace in the moonlight—to propose to her. It would be a very romantic proposal, on a summer night, with Chinese lanterns overhead and the music sounding softly over the still air.

Of course she would say yes, and by that time Papa would be here in Waveney, and she would take the young man to him, and he, of course, would be so happy to be home again that he would welcome him with all the pleasure that she could wish.

It was a dream from which she did not wake until Ella's announcement that she was engaged to Frank Sloane cut across it like a rough hand tearing away a cobweb. Only one thing was uppermost in her mind as she made her way through the already crowded rooms: she must get away from Ella and from the faithless Captain at once.

Murmuring the excuse of having to see if Bruce had been shut up to anybody who tried to detain her, she gained the comparative emptiness of the hall at last and ran across it towards the library, scarcely seeing where she was going until she was brought up sharply against a man who was standing at the foot of the stairs waiting for his sister.

'What in the world—' He caught her arm to steady her. 'Susanna!' And then, dropping his voice, conscious of the hired servants about them and the guests still arriving, 'Something or someone has upset you. What is it?'

Her eyes looked up at him desperately and he saw that they were wet with tears. 'Nothing,' she said. 'I mean, nobody. Oh please, Mr. Royde, let me go! I only came to find Bruce.'

'I can't let you go like this. You are shaking like a leaf. And there's no sign of Bruce anywhere. Take my arm and let us go on to the terrace. Quickly, before the dancing starts.' He led her through the library and out of the long windows into the coolness of the summer night, to where the great golden globes of the paper lanterns hung above the terraces among the fairy lights in the trees. She went with him meekly in the setting of her shattered dreams, her hand drawn through his arm and held in a strong grasp.

'Now,' said Edward Royde when they had reached a corner sufficiently removed from the long ballroom windows to ensure a temporary privacy—he was a man very sensitive to such things—'now tell me what has happened?'

She ought to have been furious with him for his interference, but strangely she wasn't. For the first time since she had known him he was no longer unapproachable: he was warm and human, offering support and shelter.

She stammered out, 'It's Ella. She's engaged to Cap-

121

tain S-Sloane. She showed me her ring—she did it to spite me. She knew—' She broke off on a sob.

'Control yourself, Susanna!' Edward Royde spoke sternly. 'You have got to go back into that room in a few minutes and start the dancing. You cannot possibly do it in this condition. Stop shaking and pull yourself together, there's a good child.'

His words were like a douche of cold water. She gave a gasp and took a grip on herself. 'When we were playing tennis at Mrs. Taverner's he made me p-promise to keep the f-first dance for him, and the s-supper dance,' she said through chattering teeth.

'That is easily settled. Give me your programme.' He took the pretty card from her and scoring out Captain Sloane's initials put his own there instead. The orchestras were tuning up: the first dance was imminent. He stood there with the light of the lanterns on his face, illuminating the kindness there, though she thought he looked stern as well, as if somebody had made him angry. 'No tears?'

'N-no.'

'That's a good thing. I will not dance with a weeping partner. People will think I'm treading on your toes.'

She managed a wan smile. 'B-but you don't like dancing.'

'I think I told you once that I like dancing with a congenial partner.' He held out his arm. 'Come along, child. Face the lot of them—head up and shoulders back. Don't forget *you* are the belle of this ball—not Ella Somerton! And for God's sake—*smile!*'

Beneath the Chinese lanterns, breaking the marble balustrade, statues gleamed white round the terraces, the scent of summer jasmine and honeysuckle mingling with that of the white roses with which the gardeners had filled the stone vases for that night. The moonlight lit up the scene like the setting of a stage: all her life, she thought, she would remember the moonlight and those lanterns, and instead of the romantic proposal from the faithless Sloane, Royde's voice deep and somehow comforting in spite of its brusqueness, and the anxious kindness of his face.

She put her hand into his arm once more, lifted her head proudly and walked with him to the first of the open windows of the ballroom, and as they entered it together she looked up at him and smiled and heard him say 'Well done!'

Across the crowded room Mrs. Somerton saw them come in from the terrace together and thought, 'So it's Royde she's after, the little wretch. Ella was quite mistaken in thinking it was Frank!'

12

In the meantime, up in the dressing-room that he had used for the past fortnight, Will was shaking hands with his brother, while old Bruce settled himself thankfully on the hearthrug, his tail still thumping from the delighted onset of his welcome.

'I cannot tell how thankful I am to see you back,' Will said. 'We began to think that our local Revolutionary had got you, didn't we, Jobson?'

'We were certainly worried about you, Sir John,' said Jobson.

'A Revolutionary? Down here in Waveney?' John sounded incredulous, and when Will told him about Signor Calbanisi he laughed. 'I should say he was simply trying to make some money out of you,' he said. 'I have not met many such gentlemen in England.' Jobson helped them to change clothes quickly and when it was done the Admiral said, 'I don't like this by half, Will, old fellow. I wish you would stay. I can introduce you to everybody downstairs as my twin brother just arrived from Paris.'

Will took him by the arm and led him in front of the cheval glass. 'Look!' he said. 'We are not exactly alike, and over the past fortnight or more *that* reflection is the "Admiral" as seen by your acquaintances and friends.' He made a slight gesture towards his own image. 'I am thinner than you are and paler. If I were to go downstairs with you now people would look at me and say, "But *that* is the man we have known as the Admiral!" Whereas if you re-enter the ballroom alone

124

they will possibly remark upon how well the Admiral is looking tonight and that he is considerably stouter than when he arrived home. And you will be able to walk among your guests, picking up the threads as you go. It is fortunate that we have not seen much of our relations: even Great-Aunt Margaret has suspected nothing so far.'

'I daresay you are right.' The Admiral dropped his hand affectionately on his brother's shoulder. 'But you will come back and stay here later on?'

'Thank you, John. I may indeed do that.'

The Admiral went downstairs and took up Will's old position just inside the ballroom. There was no need now to shut up Bruce in the misery of a loose-box or the kennels where the gun-dogs lived. He would not move from the dressing-room until his adored master came back to it in the small hours.

The Countess was dancing in a stately fashion with the Lord Lieutenant, and as John Farebrother stood there looking about him, Susanna saw him and Royde felt her start, while the small hand in his tightened. He followed the direction of her eyes and said in a low voice, 'Am I mistaken, or is the Admiral back?'

She looked up at him quickly. 'You—knew?' she said.

'Yes.'

'But—how?'

'I put two and two together and found they made four. Your uncle is a splendid actor but somebody had forgotten to tell him that the Admiral does not smoke.' He smiled down at her. 'Would you like to dance round to him without attracting any attention?'

'Oh—if you please!' Her eyes were shining, her lips parted, her cheeks flushed. She looked very lovely. He took her round quickly and unobtrusively to where the Admiral was standing, and stopping in front of him he said quietly: 'How do you do, Sir John? I hope you had a good journey home?'

'How d'ye do, my boy. Yes, indeed I did. Very good. Is your sister here tonight?'

'Yes. Dancing with Captain Ashworth I think. There they are, in front of the far orchestra.'

'So they are. I can see them.' And then as his eyes came back to his daughter: 'You look very beautiful, Susie my darling.'

'Miss Farebrother had the idea that *you* should be dancing the first dance with her, sir.' Royde took his partner's hand and put it into her father's, and then with a faint smile at them both he went off to find his sister.

'Nice fellow, Royde,' the Admiral said, his arm going round his daughter tenderly. 'Well, my darling, I'm home!'

'I knew it was you, Papa, directly I saw you,' she said, her face radiant. 'Oh I'm so glad you are home— in time for my ball!'

'Not so loud, my love. Your uncle did not make too bad a job of it in my absence I believe.'

'Oh no.' She was so glad to have him home that she had forgotten about her uncle and now she said, conscience-stricken. 'Has he gone yet?'

'Yes. He asked me to say goodbye to you for him.'

'Dear Uncle Will. Was the—mission—very important?'

'It was quite an important one, my love.'

'And it is all finished now?'

'Quite finished now.'

.   .   .   .   .

Dinah had seen Will leave the room after Jobson and she had guessed that John had arrived. As soon as she could she followed them and waited upstairs in her little sitting-room until after the Admiral had gone

126

downstairs. Will saw her there a few minutes later, standing in the doorway with the old canvases of his pictures stacked against the wall behind her.

'You are leaving at once?' she said.

'Yes. By the side entrance. Honeysett is there with a closed carriage and Mrs. Bess has packed a hamper for me to take with me on the train. Dear old Mrs. Bess.'

'Directly I saw Jobson speak to you I knew John was home.' She held out her hand to him. 'I could not let you go without saying goodbye.'

He did not take her hand. His eyes were resting on her smilingly and yet there was a tautness in his face she had not seen there before. 'Goodbye, my dear,' he said then gently. 'I shall think of you whenever I think of Waveney.' On an impulse he took her face in his hands, kissed her gently on the lips, and went on his way.

'Goodbye,' she whispered after him down the stairs that led to the side entrance. 'No. Not goodbye, Will. Godspeed!'

He lifted his hand carelessly and the darkness of the staircase swallowed him up.

Mrs. Beswick found Dinah still standing outside her room after he had gone. 'Why, miss,' she said, 'is anything the matter?'

'Nothing, thank you, Mrs. Beswick. I—came up for a breath of air. The rooms down there are very warm.'

'It is a warm night.' The housekeeper sounded sorrowful. 'And so the joke is ended, miss. I only hope it doesn't end in trouble for Mr. Will, as so many of his brother's jokes have ended in the past. He's too good to be treated so lightly in my opinion, but that's the master all over. He's always taken Mr. Will for granted, knowing he'll never refuse him.'

Dinah got back to the ballroom after the first dance had finished and she found herself next to Mrs. Somerton who had been telling the Countess about Ella's engagement, adding that the announcement would be in the *Morning Post* the next day. The Countess surveyed Ella and her fiancé for some minutes through her lorgnettes before making any comment and then she said she hoped Mrs. Somerton and the Bishop were pleased, in the tone of one who would have been far from pleased in the same circumstances.

'We are delighted,' said Mrs. Somerton firmly.

'Of course,' said the Countess, 'there *is* something very gratifying in getting a daughter married.' The words might have implied that it was especially gratifying when that daughter was plain and had been out for two seasons, but fortunately Mrs. Somerton did not take them that way.

'Frank is such a charming young man,' she said.

'Indeed? I know some of Miss Dudley's relations but I have never met the Sloane side of the family. They are the Devonshire Sloanes I believe.' And the lorgnettes were directed elsewhere.

Dinah found herself left with Mrs. Somerton and offered her congratulations on the engagement. 'I wonder if Susie knows?' she said.

'Oh yes. Ella told her directly we arrived, and Susie scarcely waited to congratulate her before rushing off as if the house was on fire, and we did not see her again until just before the dancing started, when she came in through those windows over there with Mr. Royde, smiling all over her face. I noticed he did not dance with her for more than a turn or two, however, before handing her over to her father. I asked him if he knew why she had rushed away and he said she had suddenly remembered that Bruce had not been shut up. Really —are there no servants to see to such things?'

'I am sure there are, but she just did not think of it,' Dinah said gently. 'It is the excitement. Don't you remember how excited Ella was two years ago?'

Mrs. Somerton said she must go and find her sister-in-law as she wanted to introduce her to the Admiral.

Dinah stood for a moment watching her niece, who at that moment was the centre of a group of young men. She had never seen the child so radiant, she thought, and yet there was a dignity about her as well, as if somebody somewhere had taught her the art of growing up. She did not seem to be unduly upset over Ella's engagement; maybe Captain Sloane was as easily forgotten as those others had been, Signor Scaravicini among them. Dear little Susie. She was having a success tonight: what a pity it was that it could not be followed by a season in London.

Her thoughts went back to Will and she wondered if she would ever see him again. If he did come back to Waveney it would be to find her gone. Susie did not need her now and in all probability the Admiral would marry again. It would not be long perhaps before Susie herself married and she might be glad of an unattached aunt to be called on in cases of emergency, but until that time came she must look around for a tiny house somewhere in Jerningham where she could live on the small income that her father had left her. Her thoughts were interrupted by the beginning of the next dance and by Captain Ashworth who came to claim her for it.

'Do I guess aright?' he said. 'Is somebody back again?'

'Yes.'

She did not sound happy and he went on, 'I suppose the guest you have been entertaining for him has not stayed?'

'No. He has left for Paris.'

'Excellent. His work was done and he would only have embarrassed John.'

She wondered why they all could only think of John and never of Will. Had he returned to be made use of and then forgotten again and sent back to the limbo of an artist brother who painted and had a studio somewhere in Paris? A dissolute man—'foot-loose and fancy-free'.

'You are very quiet,' her partner said reproachfully, and she roused herself to the small-talk expected of her.

'How charming Dorothea looks tonight,' she said smiling.

'Ah yes. She is very happy. I don't think I shall be betraying a confidence now when I tell you that the man she has been secretly engaged to for some years is now home again, and the engagement will soon be secret no longer.'

So it was Dorothea. But if so, why had the Admiral not singled out his betrothed tonight? Except for a smile and a friendly bow he had not appeared to notice her. 'Why has it been kept a secret?' she asked puzzled.

'She was afraid that his family might not approve of the marriage,' he told her. 'She is quite a lot younger than her fiancé.'

'Oh, but I am sure his family love her already,' Dinah was beginning when he caught her up with a smile.

'It is very good of you to say so, but one is always a little nervous of these first meetings.'

'First?' She did not understand.

'Yes. Paul's ship put in at Southampton yesterday and tomorrow I am taking Dorothea to London, where he is meeting us and we are travelling on to Yorkshire with him to meet his family. Dorothea has received very welcoming letters from Paul's mother, but his father is one of those gruff Yorkshire squires, and she will have to employ all her wiles on him. He wanted his only son to marry a Yorkshire girl.'

'But I am sure he will not be able to resist Dorothea,'

Dinah said. So it was not to be Dorothea for the Admiral after all. She glanced at Sir John, standing beside Lady Sare with Mrs. Taverner and Miss Dudley talking to him.

As usual the Admiral was his charming self, teasing Mrs. Taverner because she said she was too old for dancing and reminding her that she had danced into the small hours in Sydney, and then turning from her to Miss Dudley, hoping that she was keeping up her music and that he would have the pleasure of hearing her playing again soon. Complimenting the ladies on their dresses and their looks.

She wondered which of the two had reserved the supper dance for him, and as they drew near in the dance she saw the Bishop's wife bearing down on him with her sister-in-law Ruth Somerton.

That artistic creature was dressed in a loose-fitting brown velvet dress, too thick and heavy for the warm summer night. The dress was clasped round the waist by a gold chain, the square neck and the edges of the short loose sleeves being trimmed with gold embroidery in a Greek key pattern. Her sandy hair was loosely knotted so that a few stray wisps had worked free and hung about her thin face. Her rather sharp nose was ornamented by a pair of gold-rimmed spectacles, through which her pale blue eyes peered short-sightedly.

As the dance ended and Dinah and her partner joined the group round the Admiral, Miss Somerton was telling him that she had looked forward to meeting him.

'I know your brother, Admiral, Mr. Will Farebrother. You are very like him, are you not? What a wonderful artist he is. All Paris is raving about him. You must be very proud of him. And six pictures on the line in this year's Exhibition in the Royal Academy. People are saying that he can command what price he likes now for his pictures. Thousands of pounds, I believe.

131

And he is so humble about it all too. His success means nothing to him. He is still using the little attic studio where he started when he first went to Paris years ago.' Her shrill voice stopped and the Admiral smiled. If he was surprised to hear of his brother's success he did not show it.

'There are some of his paintings left here I believe,' he said. 'I must see if I cannot find a bidder for them.'

And then he broke away from the ladies to grip Ashworth's hand, saying as he did so to Dinah, 'I've never seen you in blue before, my dear. It suits you,' before going on from them to greet other old friends.

As the supper dance started, however, he found himself either by accident or design beside Lady Sare. 'This is ours, I think?' he said.

'It is not,' she said smiling. 'I can see Colonel Wicks in the doorway struggling to reach me.'

'Have you promised it to him?'

'I have.'

'But that is nonsense. Stay where you are. I will be back in a moment.' He reached the Colonel in a few strides, took his arm and said something to him which made the little man look chagrined, but at the same time he nodded and went off in the opposite direction. 'I said I would make his apologies to you, and I do,' said the Admiral, as he slipped his arm round Lady Sare's waist and took her out on to the floor.

'What magic did you use?' she asked, smiling up at him.

'I asked him to dance with my Aunt Margaret,' he said.

Her eyes followed his to where the Colonel was bowing in front of the Countess and her smile deepened. 'Oh, the poor little man!' she said. 'How unkind of you, John!'

'When I've waited for this moment for months?' he

murmured. 'We can't talk here. May I come and see you tomorrow, Cecily?'

Her eyes met his. 'I shall be in all the morning,' she said.

In the meantime Susanna was finding it charming to be the centre of so much attention that night, and it was only when Edward Royde came to claim her for the supper dance that she found herself quiet and almost shy. His dancing was very correct and very finished: remembering her behaviour earlier in the evening and how he had coped with it she had been dreading this second dance with him in case he referred to it, but he did not. He treated her as he would have treated any other grown-up young lady, talking of the theatres he had been to in London, and remarking on the excellence of the orchestras and congratulating her on her dancing. At supper he was beside her, courteous and attentive and slightly distant as always, applauding with the rest when the speeches were made and the Admiral, making one of his easy replies for his daughter, went on to refer lightly to his last voyage and looked back to his days as a midshipman when he and his old shipmate Captain Ashworth had had their first experience of the Bay of Biscay together in one of the old wooden warships. 'And two more wretched middies could not have been found,' he added with a laugh for the Captain. Susanna listened to him contented. It was good to have Papa back again and to hear him speak and not feel on tenterhooks in case the speaker should say something that would betray him to his listeners.

It had been good to have Uncle Will, though, she thought: he was gentle and kind and understanding, and during that last fortnight he had been more helpful than Papa would have been. But now he was gone and the chrysalis stage of her existence was passed and she was a young lady. She had come out and she was regarded as grown up, and life lay before her, exciting, unknown, unexplored.

'Don't you think,' the Bishop's wife whispered to her friend Miss Dudley at the far end of the top table, 'that a certain person's dress is just a little bit *outré*? I cannot think where she had it made.'

'It has a London air about it,' Miss Dudley said pensively, studying the blue taffeta opposite them. 'It is very well chosen: one wonders if it were selected with the Admiral's home-coming in view.' Her voice was acid: she had kept two dances for the Admiral, as he had asked her to at Mrs. Taverner's party, and he had not claimed one.

'You mean—Oh no!' Mrs. Somerton was positive about that. 'There never was any hint of scandal in that direction. I assure you that if there had been I would have been the first to know.'

Miss Dudley was disappointed, but she was ready to take Mrs. Somerton's word for it. She was quite sure that where scandal and gossip was concerned she would be the first to know.

In the early hours of the following morning, when the ball was over and the girls despatched to bed and the Bishop and his wife were alone together over a nightcap, she directed her criticism once more towards Susanna.

'I do hope she becomes a little steadier and more ladylike now that she is out,' she said. 'The girls were telling me some nonsense about her the other day—the little minx had been boasting that she had been kissed—by a young man!'

'I don't see any harm in that myself,' said the Bishop mildly.

'Putting ideas into the girls' heads!'

'My dear, if such ideas were not already in their heads I should think that they were not normal. And besides,' went on the Bishop thoughtfully, 'Susanna strikes me as being a very kissable girl!'

'Hector!' His wife was shocked. 'Nice girls,' she reproved him, 'do not encourage young men to kiss them —at least not before they are engaged to be married to them.'

'I seem to remember one girl who did, though,' said her husband with a twinkle in his eye. Mrs. Somerton caught the twinkle and just for a moment there was a look in her face that made her rather like the girl he was talking about.

'That's different,' she said. 'I did marry you, after all.'

'You did, my dear, for which I am extremely thankful. But don't be too censorious over little Susanna, my love. Remember she has had no mother since she was ten years old, and that the Admiral has spent such long periods away at sea that she might just as well have had no father either.'

'I am not being censorious,' said his wife, and there was a kinder note in her voice. 'But—' She did not end her sentence and he did not ask her to: perhaps he guessed the thoughts that were in her mind.

Their poor plain Ella had managed to secure herself a husband at last, but they both secretly wished that her future husband could have been more mature and stable. And Maud, when it was her turn to come out, even if she were dressed in white satin and hundreds of pounds spent on her dress, would never look as lovely as Susanna had looked that night. Mrs. Somerton was unhappily aware that the young men who would dance with Maud would do it from a sense of duty and that she would never draw them like a magnet as Susanna had done.

She was afraid that her husband was right and that Susanna was a very kissable girl.

13

Dinah had been conscious of a feeling of numbness all the night after Will had gone. She was aware of smiling and talking, with the energy that the small-talk of a ballroom required. She heard Lady Sare complimenting her on her dress and on Susanna's, on the flowers in the rooms, on the orchestras and the supper, which she assured her could not have been bettered by any London caterer.

'There was only one thing missing in all the speeches and toasts in the supper-room,' she had added, smiling. 'Nobody mentioned you. I was quite angry about it, knowing what a lot had rested on your shoulders.' Her glance here strayed to the Countess. 'So much to arrange, so much anxiety lest things should not go right. But everything has gone right, has it not? Nothing could have been better done. You have every right to feel happy tonight.'

Happy, with Will gone? And perhaps never to come back. The numbness spread a little as Dinah smiled and thanked her friend for her kindness and said that she was indeed happy that Susanna was having such a splendid ball.

It was five o'clock before it was over, the summer sun coming up over the trees in the park, and the last of the carriages rolling away through the gates, and the last of the guests who were staying at Waveney finally going upstairs to bed.

Dinah went with Susanna to see her into bed. 'Have you enjoyed it, darling?' she asked.

'So much. It has been the loveliest ball in the world.' Susanna flung her arms round her aunt's neck. 'Did you enjoy it too, Aunt Di?'

'Yes, my darling. I am always happy when you are happy.' Little Susanna, grown up, and not needing her for very much longer. She helped her off with the lovely dress and got her undressed and into bed and left her with a final kiss. 'Sleep well, and sweet dreams.'

Sweet dreams. Susanna lay for a time listening to the songs of the birds outside her windows and somehow she could see most clearly, as she looked back on that night, Royde's stern face and hear the brusqueness in his voice as he told her to pull herself together. Yet as well there was the memory of the grasp of his hand on her arm, comforting, compelling and giving her strength to turn her back on the fairy-tale dreams of her childhood and to go back with him into the ballroom for that first dance.

Dinah went down to the empty ballroom and stood there for a few minutes looking about her. The orchestras had departed, taking their instruments with them in the Waveney station omnibus, to catch the milk-train back to London. The hundreds of candles in the great chandeliers were extinguished, the plant stands were full of wilting flowers, and the daylight came flooding through the long windows, giving the ballroom a queer, unusual light, like a stage on which the curtain has been rung down while the scene-shifters waited in the wings. The floor still shone through the faint scratches of the many feet that had danced there, and here she saw a carnation dropped from a buttonhole, there a dance programme with the pencil gone, and she picked up a lady's handkerchief, trimmed with Honiton lace and scented with eau-de-Cologne.

137

She found that the numbness was passing, that feeling was coming back, and she knew that it must not do that until the next twenty-four hours had gone and the Admiral's relatives departed to their homes. Only then could she allow herself the luxury of feeling and of grief, when they were alone again at Waveney, she and John and Susanna. The same as it had been for years, and yet not the same. Never the same again.

She went upstairs slowly and she only let the maid unhook the blue dress for her before sending her off to bed, saying that she would manage the rest for herself.

The girl went and putting on a wrapper she went into the little sitting-room next door. Here she drew up the Venetian blinds and sat for a time in the early light of the morning, looking at the pictures stacked against one wall. When the last of the guests had left Waveney she would walk across the park to old Rowlands the estate carpenter's cottage, and she would arrange for him to make a crate large enough to hold the canvases and she would have them sent to Will in Paris.

There were not very many of them. And then she saw that there was something else there with them—a folding travelling desk, exactly like the one that John always took with him to sea. She pulled it out from beside the pictures and on the lid there were Will's initials and his name, inscribed as John's were on a small brass plate let into the walnut. There were brass corners to the desk, and a key was dangling from one of the handles by a piece of string.

After a moment's hesitation she took the key off the handle and opened the lid and inside there were the same divisions for writing paper and pens and a small bottle of ink in a round red leather travelling case, with a hinged lid that fitted tightly. There was the same slanting writing board covered in tooled green leather, and under it a few old letters, some tied with ribbon.

'Love-letters,' she thought. 'A schoolboy's passion.' And then as she looked at them again she saw that they were addressed to him in her sister's handwriting.

Mary! But it was not possible. She had hated John's brother. Would these letters explain her dislike for him perhaps?

Guiltily and hating herself for doing it, she opened the letters and to her astonishment she found that they were love-letters from a woman who had signed herself in every one of them except the last: *Your loving wife to be, Mary.*

The last letter was very different: in it she said that she had made a mistake, and that it was no good for him to be angry with her. She had thought it over and she had made up her mind that she could not marry a man who was poor. She had been poor all her life and she hated it, and so she was going to marry his brother instead. Nobody knew that they had been engaged— least of all John—and though she was not in love with him he was in love with her, and she would trust to Will not to betray her. There would be Waveney to live in when their parents were gone, and she would have money to spend and a position in the world.

On the envelope Will had written: *She kept my ring, she married my brother, and when I went to Waveney for my Mother's funeral she told me I was never to go there again. What a queer sense of values some women have.*

The date on that letter was the year that Mary married John, and looking back Dinah remembered that her sister had been staying with their father's sister, their Aunt Euphemia, in London for six months or so during the previous year to have singing lessons from one of Aunt Phemie's pet singers. She had prided herself on encouraging talented young people, artists, writers, singers, even actors and actresses. Mary had had lessons from a pupil of Madame Adeline Patti herself.

At the end of that six months Mary had come home in a state of dreamy expectancy and happiness, watching the post for letters, writing some herself and posting them without putting them out for her father to stamp for her. At the end of that year Aunt Phemie had asked her there again to continue her singing lessons, and it was then that she had met John and got engaged to him in the space of three weeks.

No wonder Waveney had such bitter memories for Will. She tied up the letters again and thrust them down into the desk under a small pile of notes on painting. Then she locked the desk, tied the key on to the handle again, and went back to bed.

But not to sleep. She thought, as she lay there with her mind on Mary, that she would never be able to sleep again.

14

Will caught the midnight train to London, arriving at the Métropole in Northumberland Avenue at four o'clock in the morning. As the hotel management prided itself on having the place open and ready for its guests at any hour of the day and night, there was no difficulty in getting a room, and he found it singularly comfortable to be able to use his own name again.

After a short sleep, followed by a visit from the hotel barber, a bath and breakfast, he felt a great deal refreshed, and at half past ten he made his way out to Putney on the London and South Western Railway.

His aunt's house was a large stuccoed villa with a carriage way in front and a long garden sloping down to the river at the back. It was a house that had needed half a dozen servants in the old days, and Mrs. Duncombe now had two beside her companion, Miss Macdonald, a Scotswoman who had managed to put up with her for over ten years.

There was a daily gardener for the garden and the small coach-house held nothing but an old and shabby landau. When Mrs. Duncombe drove out she hired a horse and driver from the nearest livery stables.

The house-parlourmaid who answered the door was a stranger to Will and told him doubtfully that Mrs. Duncombe did not usually receive visitors in the morning unless they were relatives or old friends.

'I am her nephew,' he reassured the girl, and gave her

his card to take to his aunt, and while she went off with it she left him to cool his heels in the drawing-room.

It was an apartment much as he remembered it, in fact he had never known it to change since the first time he had come on a visit there when he was seven years old. John had contracted scarlet fever and their aunt had offered to take Will so that he should not catch it from his brother.

It smelt now rather as if the windows had not been opened for years, but he looked about him with nostalgic satisfaction, noting the treasures that had fascinated him as a small boy.

There was the ostrich egg that somebody had brought Mrs. Duncombe from abroad, the fan of peacock feathers in the empty grate—the feathers a little moulting now perhaps—the mahogany firescreen worked in hideous Berlin wools in shades of purple, mauve and green, the marble statue of Minerva on its ebony stand, the potted palm—could it be the same one?—in the brass jardiniére on the octagonal table in the bay window. And surely those were the same green serge curtains, with their edging of green woollen balls, and the same Nottingham lace ones inside them to screen the windows? The brass lamp with its fluted pink shade stood on the bureau in the position it had always held, and beyond the bureau the upright piano had new candles in the brass holders, and the music stool was there, with the green plush seat on which that distant small boy had amused himself one wet Sunday afternoon by swivelling round and round until he felt sick.

Nothing had altered, and memories came back thick and fast as he sat waiting for his aunt, and then there came the sound of voices, and a stick tapping on the hall floor, and the door opened and Mrs. Duncombe came in.

She was dressed in a purple serge dress, cut as her

142

dresses always had been, with flowing skirt and braided bodice and long, close-fitting sleeves, a lace jabot pinned with a French cameo at her throat, and a lace cap, with purple velvet ribbons, on her scanty white hair.

Her eyes were bright with interest and alive with affection and although she had become more shrunken and looked very frail, her voice was as strong as ever as she greeted him.

'My dearest boy!' She held out her hand and he took it gently and kissed her wrinkled cheek, the skin soft as powder under his lips. 'This is an unexpected joy. What brings you to England, my dear? Your pictures? You have come over to see them I suppose. It was a proud moment for me when our Vicar here told me about them. "Macdonald," I said, "we must go to the Academy. We must see Will's pictures." I sent a note to the livery stables, and the gardener cleaned up the carriage and we set out, didn't we, Macdonald? And there was your name in the catalogue, and there were your pictures on the line. Such fine pictures, Will, and so wonderfully painted. You should have heard the remarks of the people as they came and looked at them. "Oh," they said, "William Farebrother. That's the new artist, isn't it? Aren't they excellent?" I was so proud of you. You have come a long way since the days when you went round the countryside painting farmers' wives.' She chuckled and made him sit down beside her on the settee in front of the grate with its peacock-feather fan. 'I always remember what you told me about those days. You would see a farmer's wife feeding her chickens and you would ask if you could paint her picture and she would tell you to come back the next day. And when you returned there she would be, all dressed up in her best with her hair in corkscrew curls and a locket as big as a soup-plate round her neck.'

'But as the portrait was intended for the best parlour,'

he protested, 'naturally she wanted to wear her parlour dress.'

He sat and talked to her, leading her away from his pictures and towards Waveney and John, but she dismissed both without exhibiting any gratitude for the generosity her elder nephew was showing her. She made him stay to midday dinner, which consisted of a leg of mutton and onion sauce, followed by rice pudding, which once more took him back to his childhood, and she insisted on having a bottle of sour claret opened for him and he drank it bravely, trying not to think of the havoc it would play with his stomach. He never could drink sour wines.

Afterwards he sat for a time with her in the garden while she told him of her plans for him.

'When I die,' she told him, 'thanks to that horrid bank I shall not have a fortune to leave you—as I had once. There will only be this house and its contents. I had plans for building a studio for you at the bottom of the garden. There is plenty of room for it there, and the walls between this garden and those on either side are high and thick. You would have found it quiet there and nobody would have disturbed you. But now you are famous you will be moving to some smart district, I daresay—like St. John's Wood or Kensington. I understand that Sir Frederick Leighton's studio there has glass sides and roof.' She sighed and then she patted his hand and smiled at him. 'Putney is not fashionable enough for you now, my dear.'

'Aunt Clara, you know me better than that. Can you see me in smart and fashionable circles? I have always been content to paint my humble world as I see it, and I shall continue to do so, however many pictures I sell.'

'And you are really making money now?'

'I sold the copyrights of my last picture for six thousand pounds.'

144

She seemed to understand that and be satisfied with it. Then she said abruptly: 'You are not married?'

'No.'

'You should marry. Have you not met anybody you wanted to marry?'

He hesitated. 'Not until the past fortnight,' he said then reluctantly. 'I met her first many years ago, and when we met again I designed a ball-dress for her—in French blue.'

'What is she like?'

He did not say that she knew her already. He said gently: 'She is tall and dark, with smoke-grey eyes that were made suddenly blue by the French blue of the dress. She—looked very beautiful in it.'

'You speak as if you were in love with her.'

'I believe I may be.' He smiled and her sharp eyes caught the tenderness in his face.

'Then you cannot afford to waste any more time,' she said severely. 'Go and ask her.'

'Maybe I will, when I have finished all I have to do here.' There was the lawyer to see again, and the bank manager in London, and arrangements to be made to pay back that ten thousand to Waveney. And there were the sales of his pictures to be noted and appreciated, and more copyrights to be signed. And then he must go back to Paris, to clear up his studio and to find somewhere else to live—probably in London. There was plenty of time, he thought, as he took the boat train to Dover a few days later. But whether it was to be London, or the outskirts of Paris, or a country cottage in England or in France, the thought of settling down with Dinah as his wife was becoming more attractive every day.

．　　．　　．　　．　　．

On the morning after the ball the Admiral took leave of those of his guests who were leaving that day as soon as they were assembled for breakfast. He had told Honeysett to have carriages ready for any who wished to catch the London train from Jerningham, and he added that if the rest wished to stay at Waveney until after the Jubilee on the following week they were welcome to do so.

As most of his guests had seats booked *en route* to see the processions, however, and some of them, like himself, were taking part in the processions, and as London promised to be gay and inviting, his offers of the carriages were gladly accepted, and Perryman was besieged for *Bradshaw's Railway Guide*. Directly the Admiral had seen the Countess—the first to leave—to her carriage he left the rest to be seen off by Dinah and Susanna, and took himself off on a new chestnut brought over from Colonel Wicks for him to try. Once clear of the gates he turned its head towards Royde Park, and having arrived at that hospitable mansion, was told that Lady Sare was at home. She was waiting to greet him in her sitting-room upstairs, and as she got up he came to her quickly and took her hands in his.

'How was Her Highness?' she asked.

'Delighted to see her small son again, as you may imagine.' He kept her hands in his for a moment and then she drew them away and motioned to him to sit beside her on the settee in the window.

'Tell me about it,' she said. 'Was it difficult?'

'Not really. In fact it was quite simple. Your brother's yacht was waiting for me just outside Marseilles, with the Princess on board. I took the boat down to the Adriatic, where the child was being kept virtually a prisoner in a castle belonging to his grandmother. The Princess had learned, however, that he was taken by his

146

nurse down to a deserted strip of beach every morning.
Nobody was allowed near this beach, and there were
armed guards round it. I sent in a reconnoitring party
and we discovered that the guards did not number more
than half a dozen, if that, but that they were armed. So
we anchored outside the bay, flying your brother's
pennant and looking as much as we could like a private
yacht's company on pleasure bent. Then at night, unwilling to waste more time, I sent in a landing party,
and in the morning while the guards were playing Nap
or Boule or whatever it is they play in those parts, with
their rifles stacked neatly in an unguarded pile, my men
overpowered them, trussed them up and gave us the
signal to come in. I took a boat in, took the child and
his nurse aboard and made them lie flat in the bottom
of the boat covered by a rug in case somebody put a
telescope on us from the castle, and made my way back
to the yacht, where Her Highness was waiting. Then it
was a case of running up the White Ensign, up anchor
and away. My passengers are now happily quartered at
Windsor on their way to Balmoral, where a fond and
august relative awaits them.' He paused. 'You know a
great deal about it, don't you, Cecily?'

'I have known the Princess for years,' she said. 'And
I was not the only one to be horrified when she was
married off at eighteen to that brute. I heard nothing of
her after the wedding, until last year when there was
a rumour going round that she had left him. And then
I met her again at a dinner-party in London last March.
I could see that she was worried and upset, and although she was very kind and talked to me as we have
always talked together, there was something of which
she could not speak and I thought it must be to do with
the child. I happened to see my brother-in-law the next
day and I asked him about it—he is in the Admiralty,
as you know—and he said that the Prince was vir-

tually holding the boy hostage hoping to bring his wife to her knees. But he has been so brutal to her that she could not go back to him, and Chevington asked me if I knew a man with a knowledge of the sea who would be resourceful enough to fetch the boy from what was virtually the lion's mouth. I thought of you at once, and he said you were the very man and that he would send for you directly you landed at Portsmouth.'

'Which he did,' he said smiling. 'And fortunately it is a story that has had a happy ending.'

'Yes,' said Lady Sare. 'I don't think the Prince will dare to send any of his paid miscreants to England after them.'

'Will he not?' For a fleeting moment he thought of Will and the Italian gentleman he had locked up in the gamekeeper's hut, and then he looked at Lady Cecily and forgot all about it. Her hand was on the settee between them and he covered it with his own. 'I wrote to you from Sydney,' he reminded her. 'I told you I would have something to ask you when I got home. Did you guess what it was?'

'I think so,' she said. There was no coquetry about her.

'Will you marry me, Cecily?' he asked. 'There's nobody I'd sooner have as the mistress of Waveney—and I don't think you will find it difficult to get on with Susanna. She is an affectionate child—if somewhat spoiled.'

'But I love Susanna,' she said. Her hand turned upwards in his, and she leant forward and kissed him. 'Don't look so anxious, John. I love you too—and that is all that matters.'

It seemed that whatever Mrs. Somerton might think to the contrary, the Admiral was very well able to choose a wife for himself. Later she asked him what they were going to do with Dinah. 'She has been at

Waveney so long that she must look on it as her home.'

'Oh, I'll build her a house in the village,' he said carelessly. 'She teaches in the Sunday school and is always taking jellies and things like that to the villagers if they are ill. She is full of good works and she will enjoy being nearer the church.'

She wondered if he dismissed Dinah so easily because she reminded him of his first wife.

Jubilee Day dawned—the loveliest day of that lovely summer. From an early hour good-tempered crowds had gathered in the London streets and the stands were filling fast. The bronze lions in Trafalgar Square were crammed with people and the shrouds and halyards of the barges at anchor along the Embankment were full of girls and boys, hanging on like seagulls to see the Queen.

The route of the procession was a long one: from Buckingham Palace up Constitution Hill to Hyde Park Corner, along Piccadilly, down Regent Street into Waterloo Place, and thence to Pall Mall. From there it travelled through Cockspur Street into Northumberland Avenue to the Victoria Embankment and then on to Westminster Bridge, down Bridge Street and round St. Margaret's churchyard to the Broad Sanctuary and the west doors of the Abbey.

The Admiral's family had seats at the upper windows of Lord Chevington's house and there Lady Sare and Susanna and Mr. Royde were joined by some of the Chevingtons, one of the boys, aged fifteen, monopolising Susanna, taking the vacant seat beside her and explaining to her in detail each procession that passed. She had to listen as politely as she could, while her whole attention was not on the endless processions, but on the silent figure of Edward Royde, standing in the shadowy room behind them. She could have cheerfully strangled the gregarious schoolboy beside her.

149

For half an hour before the Queen left the Palace the processions before hers went on ahead: there were Emperors and Empresses in it, Kings and Queens, Princes and Princesses, Grand Dukes and Duchesses, Maharajahs in bright silks and glittering jewels, governors from the colonies, potentates from Japan, South Africa and the Pacific Islands. There were Ambassadors, soldiers and sailors who were the nation's heroes, robed officers of State, equerries and ladies-in-waiting, and each procession had its outriders, its escort and its band from a famous regiment. And right at the end of all those other processions, preceded by a cavalcade of seventeen Princes, nine of them being grandsons or the husbands of the grand-daughters of Her Majesty and three of them her own sons, riding three abreast, and followed immediately by an Indian escort, there came six cream-coloured horses drawing an open carriage with a small, plump old lady in it under a parasol.

But long before the Queen had left the Palace while all those other processions were passing down Piccadilly Susanna had felt a touch on her arm and found Edward Royde beside her.

'I think if you look at the next carriage,' he said in a low voice, 'the carriage with the lady and the little boy in it—you will see your father riding on the far side.'

She looked eagerly. 'Yes,' she said. 'There is Papa. Who is the little fair-haired boy? He seems to be talking to Papa as if he knows him very well. And the lady—she is smiling at him now.'

'I expect she is one of Her Majesty's relatives from one of the smaller German states,' Royde said. 'She has many such relations I believe.'

'Papa has saluted the little boy and the lady and he is dropping behind them, and now some troopers have come forward to ride on either side of the carriage. The little boy must be rather important to be guarded so well.'

'We always guard our foreign royalties,' Royde said. 'It is only our own Queen who goes about with a parasol in her hand and her soldiers and sailors before her and behind.'

The procession with the little fair-haired boy and the Admiral moved on and out of sight, being immediately replaced by another of grandees from Spain and Portugal, and Susanna lost interest. Edward Royde moved back away from her into the shadowy room and the garrulous schoolboy beside her explained how he knew the uniforms of Portugal from those of Spain. Susanna thought that when he grew up he would make an excellent Prime Minister or Chancellor of the Exchequer. Once on his feet in the House he would never be contradicted or argued with by anybody because the spate of his words and totally unnecessary explanations would have sent all his listeners to sleep from sheer boredom.

.   .   .   .   .

That same evening Will Farebrother was putting the finishing touches to a picture of Dinah at Waveney when there was a knock on his studio door. He opened it to find the Italian whom he had last seen in the gamekeeper's hut: the man was looking wilder than usual, he had been drinking heavily and the grin on his face was extremely unpleasant.

'So I have tracked you down at last!' he cried. 'And here you are, waiting for me and my revenge. Nobody insults Mario Calbanisi without paying for it, and I have brought something with me this time that will settle my account with you for ever.' He whipped out a pistol from behind his back and fired: at such short range he could scarcely miss.

15

Dinah had been left behind at Waveney at her own request to superintend the village children's fête in the park. There were about a hundred there, coming mostly from the cottages of the estate workers. It was a beautiful day and the tables were spread with buns and fruit and lemonade. Races were run and the boys had a cricket match, under the stern eye of Jobson who had been a great cricketer in his youth, and for the girls there were skipping contests and rounders. And at the end of it every child received a silver sixpence from the Admiral, distributed by Dinah.

It was a happy day for Waveney, ending up with every cottage window being lighted by transparencies, and all with the Queen's portrait there to show their loyalty.

Dinah walked back across the park alone. Now that the busy day was done her thoughts were free to go back over the past fortnight and to Will, and to her sister and her treatment of him. After the Admiral had married Lady Sare she did not suppose she would see Will again.

She was happy to think though that Cecily was to be John's wife because it meant that Susanna's future would be in kindly, capable hands. Lady Sare was already talking of taking her abroad to show her Paris and Italy, and the Paris and Italy she would show the child would be that of British society abroad. Ella Somerton was welcome to Captain Sloane, and Dinah felt that Susanna might have had a narrow escape, but knowing nothing of Will's conversation with the Captain during Mrs. Taverner's garden-party, she did find herself wondering at the inconstancy of the young man.

As for herself, she had no desire to stay at Waveney: she could only wish now to leave it as soon as possible. Thirty-five was too old to think of marriage, and there was only one man she could consider in that way and he had never thought of her, of that she was very sure. An artist, he had created a lovely dress for her, and then he had gone on his way, lightly touching her lips in passing in a caress that meant nothing at all.

The house seemed very empty when she arrived back at the Manor. Perryman was waiting for her and she missed Susanna's eager chattering, and the Admiral's careless kindly greeting.

'I think the children enjoyed themselves, Perryman,' she said.

'I am sure they did, miss. I have put a light supper in your sitting-room: Mrs. Beswick thought you would prefer it up there, seeing as you are alone.'

'Thank you, Perryman. It was thoughtful of her. I will ring if I want anything but I am sure I shall not.'

She went upstairs while Perryman went back to the cosiness of the housekeeper's room, where some of Mrs. Beswick's best mulberry wine, with the body and bouquet of madeira, waited for him to join her in toasting Her Majesty.

Dinah ate her solitary meal thinking back over the past years since she had come to take charge of Mary's child. They had been happy, busy years, if the servants had treated her as a superior governess, while the Admiral had shown her the careless hospitality which he would have extended to any other dependent relation. He knew that her brother, the present squarson of the village where the Woodcock family had lived for generations, had nothing to spare for an unmarried sister, and as she was living at Waveney at the Admiral's expense he had every right to treat her as he chose. She had not appreciated her position fully in the household, however, until Will came, with his face that was so like his brother's, and the gentle considerate manner that was so widely different. Will had time for people's troubles and a great understanding of their problems where John would dismiss them with a laugh or a shrug.

As Dorothea had helped her at the fête that day they had talked of what her father was going to do when she married.

Captain Ashworth had decided to move to a charming little house on the river front at Strand-on-the-Green, where he could see boats passing up and down the Thames and take a boat out himself when he felt inclined. His manservant—another old salt—was to go with him and together they would enjoy their bachelor existence, without being troubled by any women except perhaps for a cook and a housemaid. 'My brother and his family will be near him too,' Dorothea added. 'Which will delight my father. He adores his grandchildren.'

'He is not going to move to Jerningham then? There is a riverside there.'

'I know. But I think he is mortally afraid of the Bishop's wife, in case she selects a wife for him as she tried to do for the Admiral. He does not intend to marry again.' She paused for a moment and then continued: 'I am sorry in a way. I would have liked him to have some nice sensible creature with him—somebody like you, Dinah. But he will not hear of it.'

'He is in no danger from me.' Dinah had laughed and turned the conversation to Dorothea's wedding, only a fortnight away, to be followed the next week by the Admiral's, at which the whole village coupled with

Royde would again be *en fête*, in fact a great deal more excitement could be expected then than for the Jubilee.

Three days after the Jubilee two telegrams arrived at Waveney, needing the Admiral's immediate attention. One informed him that his Aunt Clara had died suddenly of a heart attack in Putney, and the second was from the Embassy in Paris, telling him that his brother had been shot by an assassin and was lying gravely ill in a French hospital.

The Admiral's portmanteau was packed and Jobson was standing in the hall ready to accompany him to Putney to arrange for Mrs. Duncombe's funeral when the second telegram arrived, and John Farebrother stared from it to Dinah with a stupefied air. The carriage was waiting to take him to Jerningham station to catch the London train: there was the old lady to bury at the other end, and yet here was his brother, who might be dying. He was torn between the two.

Dinah did not know how he could hesitate, but seeing that he did she had a suggestion to make. 'Supposing I go to Paris for you?' she said quietly. 'Then you will be free to go to Putney. There is nobody to see to Mrs. Duncombe's funeral but you: she was your father's sister and you are her nearest relation, and I cannot see any members of the family who were here recently caring a straw for her. It will not take me long to pack what I need, and perhaps Lady Sare would have Susanna to stay at Royde Park while we are both away.'

'But you cannot travel to Paris alone.' The Admiral was eager to snatch at this easy way of solving his problem however, and Dinah saw it and continued quickly:

'I travelled alone from Perth when Mary died and things are much easier now. I am no young girl, John. I can manage very well on my own.'

Susanna had no wish to stay at Royde Park. 'I do

not see why Mr. Copthorne could not arrange the funeral for you, Papa,' she said.

'I never said he couldn't, but I would like to be there when the will is opened, because I think the old lady left all she had to your uncle, and I do not want Copthorne or any other lawyer to have too many pickings from what little there is. Much as I would like to be with dear old Will if he is as bad as this telegram says, I feel I cannot speed his recovery by being at his bedside, while I could do him a great deal more good by looking after his interests here at home.'

'Then if Aunt Dinah goes to Paris,' Susanna said, 'I shall go with her.'

'Nonsense, child!' The Admiral's quarter-deck voice came into play. 'That is ridiculous.'

As by that time it was too late to set out for the train he had planned to catch, the carriage was ordered to go to Royde Park instead, with an imperious summons to Lady Sare to come at once. She came, and when the situation was explained to her she said that she thought it not at all ridiculous that Susanna should accompany her aunt.

'Susanna speaks excellent French,' she said. 'I have heard her talking to Miss Bentley, the Bishop's governess. Whereas I rather doubt if Miss Woodcock speaks it at all?'

Dinah had to admit that her knowledge of the language was elementary.

'And as in France the people have the unfortunate habit of speaking French,' Lady Sare continued serenely, 'especially in hospitals and places like that, I think it would be wise for Miss Woodcock to have an interpreter with her. And if you still object to two females travelling so far alone and taking hotel rooms for themselves in that wicked city of Paris, then, my dearest John, I think I can persuade my brother to be

156

their escort. This is the time of year when Edward pays one of his visits to Paris—to help an old friend to keep an anniversary—and I do not think for one moment he will object to travelling a week or so earlier than usual.'

On being approached Edward Royde expressed his willingness to escort the ladies, and when the Admiral left for Putney that afternoon it was with the feeling that he had done all he could to help his brother.

On the following morning the three of them set out —an ill-matched trio, Susanna felt unhappily—with Mr. Royde's servant Floyd, and Mrs. Beswick's niece Jessie, who was to act as maid to the two ladies, bringing up the rear.

The Channel was rough as they left Dover in the late afternoon, and almost immediately Dinah and Jessie were forced to go below deck and submit to the ministrations of the stewardess. Susanna stayed happily on deck, leaning on the rail beside Royde.

'I am enjoying this,' she told him, her eyes sparkling. 'I think I must take after Papa.' In her sailor hat with its blue ribbons and the short blue jacket over her travelling dress she was like a child on holiday. She looked, he thought, delightfully young.

'It only takes an hour an a half before we are again on dry land,' he told her. 'And the sea is more choppy than rough—nothing to a good sailor.'

She wished she could recapture something of the warmth and friendliness that he had shown her on the night of her ball, but except for the moment when they were watching the Jubilee processions, he had shown no interest in her whatever. He was as distant now as he had ever been. She sighed and the sparkle died as her thoughts went back to her uncle.

'It must have been that Italian, I suppose,' she said, speaking her thoughts aloud. 'He wanted Uncle Will to give him some money and he refused, but because

157

Papa was not at home and might be in danger from the man's friends, he and Jobson shut him up in the game-keeper's hut. But he escaped and they never saw him again.'

Edward Royde had not heard about this. 'What was he like?' he asked.

'I don't know. He came at night when we were all in bed—all, that is to say, except Uncle Will. He said he was a Revolutionary.'

'Did he indeed?' Royde frowned. The Admiral, he thought, when he insisted on taking his brother from his studio to impersonate him at Waveney had shown a remarkable disregard for his safety.

'Uncle Will did not want any of us to know, but I wormed it out of Richards—he is the head gamekeeper, and he made me promise not to tell anyone in case it was a danger to Papa.' She shook her head. 'And all the time it was not Papa who was in danger, but dear Uncle Will. I do hope—he will recover.'

'There are excellent doctors in Paris and the Ambassador will see that he has the best. Try not to worry too much.' He spoke kindly and no doubt intended to be reassuring but the friend she had found on the night of her ball still seemed to be a very long way off.

On their arrival in Paris that evening he conducted them to the Hôtel du Palais in the Champs-Elysées and engaged bedrooms and a salon for them and a room for their maid. Almost immediately Dinah went to bed, exhausted after the strain of the past few weeks culminating in this added worry over Will and the journey, and Susanna was left with Mr. Royde in the elegant salon, with its splendid crimson velvet curtains and gilt chairs.

'I hope you will be comfortable here,' he said. 'It is a good hotel and the service is excellent. Do not hesitate to order anything you need.'

'I will not.' She tried to be as distant as he was and

failed. 'Mr. Royde, you have been so very kind, but there is no reason why we should keep you from your friends any longer. We shall manage here very well.'

'I am in no hurry,' he said more gently. He looked out of the window at the street lamps trailing off like a string of pearls into the darkness. 'Paris is a city that I both love and hate,' he said in a low voice. 'I have had my happiest moments in it and my saddest.' He turned his head and saw her looking at him, her lips parted, her eyes puzzled but warm with sympathy, and he smiled constrainedly. 'Forgive me. We are both tired, I think. Would you like me to drive on to the Embassy now and find the latest report on your uncle? I will send you a note if there is good news to impart, so that you may go to bed feeling a little happier.'

'Oh yes. Thank you.' What a strange man he was—at one moment so unapproachable and the next so warm and human. She did not know what to make of him. He said good night abruptly and went away and an hour or so later, just as she was about to go to bed a hotel servant brought her a letter. *My dear Miss Farebrother*, Royde had written in a firm hand that was somehow like himself. *The bullet has been removed from your uncle's shoulder and although he has fever and the next few days must be critical I am assured there is every hope he will survive. He has an excellent doctor and the French Sisters of Mercy are the best nurses in the world. But I have no doubt when a tonic is allowed the sight of you and your aunt will be all that he will need. I will only add that if you want me at any time you have only to send. I shall be at the Grand Hôtel in the Boulevard des Capucines. Yours. E. R.*

While the formal beginning of the letter might have emphasised his recognition of her new status in the world it was on the whole comforting and kind. She was a little surprised to find that he too was staying in

159

a hotel and not with his friends, but she took the letter to her aunt and was delighted to see how much better she looked when she had read it. 'You are very fond of Uncle Will, aren't you, Aunt Di?' she said.

'He is a very wonderful man,' Dinah said steadily, disregarding the implications in Susanna's question. 'It would have been too cruel if after all these years of struggle he was to die now—when he has only just tasted success.'

'He won't die,' Susanna said confidently. 'Mr. Royde will not let him die. You will see.' She kissed her aunt in the way of a mother comforting her child and went away, and Dinah lay for a time thinking about her. Darling Susie. But she must not fall in love with Royde. She was much too young for him and he would not give her a second thought. Besides there was gossip about him and his friend in Paris. Mrs. Somerton had always hinted at it, but never actually said that he was understood to have a mistress there. Yet had that been so would Lady Sare have been so ready to put them in his care on the journey? She had spoken quite openly of an old friend and an anniversary, and what would Mrs. Somerton make out of that? It was a question she was too tired to answer that night.

.　　.　　.　　.　　.

The next day Royde called for them early and took them to visit the hospital, and after Susanna had pleaded with Authority in a boat-shaped cap, putting everything she had behind a voluble stream of French, they were finally allowed to see the patient *pour un moment —mais seulement un moment, madame*.

They were taken quietly down a long ward to where a man lay motionless, his left shoulder and arm strapped with bandages.

160

'The assassin's bullet missed his heart by a hair's breadth. It was only by the mercy of God that he is alive.' So the Sister whispered to Susanna and she translated it to Dinah, while the three of them stood beside Will's bed. His eyes were closed, the fair lashes long on his cheek, his beard losing its imperial shape in a stubble spreading over his chin. 'The doctors say that he must not have excitement of any kind,' the Sister went on. 'Strangers and friends are not allowed to visit him, only relatives. You are his niece, mademoiselle?'

'Yes.'

'And this lady?'

'Not a relative—as yet,' Susanna said.

'Ah! His fiancée. The doctors will not mind that.'

Susanna took her aunt away, promising that they would come again on the following day. Their positions had now been reversed: Dinah depended upon her to be guided and helped and comforted because she was the stronger of the two.

For Dinah the next week or so passed in a dream, composed of daily visits to the hospital and thankfulness when at the end of the day Susanna came to fetch her and she could know that he was holding his own. The Sister seemed content for her to stay and help in small ways to nurse him. She did not know what Susanna did with her time, because after a peep at her uncle and a few words with the Sister she would disappear until the evening. As for Dinah, her whole world was now in that hospital bed and she knew that if Will were to die she would not want to live. The old numbness had come back making her blind and deaf to all else, in her mind the echo of the housekeeper's words on the night when he had left Waveney. 'The Admiral's always taken Mr. Will for granted, knowing he'll not refuse him.' And her grim hope that now the Admiral's joke was ended it would not mean trouble for his brother.

161

The Admiral had always had his way, brushing aside protests with an arrogance linked with the certainty that nothing he wished to do could be impossible. It made him no doubt a splendid officer in Her Majesty's service, but ruthless where his family and friends were concerned.

In the meantime it was Susanna who wrote daily reports on her uncle's health to her father. *The doctors say he is stronger,* she wrote. *I confess that I cannot see it yet and neither I think can Aunt Di, but I do not stay with him at all. I leave Aunt Di to help the Sisters with his nursing.*

The week dragged by and at last there came a day when as Dinah approached the bed she saw that its occupant's eyes were open and as their gaze rested upon her she saw a smile touch his lips.

'I thought it must be you,' he said. 'They told me my fiancée was here every day and I could not think at first who it could be.'

'That was Susie,' she said quickly, colouring up. 'She told me, little monkey, that unless she could provide them with some sort of relationship for me, they would not let me stay and nurse you, and it was all she could think of in a hurry.'

'I am glad I have such a resourceful niece,' he said gravely, and as her eyes met his the numbness suddenly passed. She sat down on the chair by his bed. 'That's better,' he said. 'Now tell me everything that has happened at Waveney since I left.'

She told him about the Admiral's engagement to Lady Sare and also of Mrs. Duncombe's death, neither of which seemed to surprise him very much.

'I thought poor old Aunt Clara could not last much longer.' He told her about the house in Putney with its long garden down to the river and the studio his aunt had planned to build for him there. Then he fell silent,

162

content to lay there and look at her: he would paint her in the dress she had worn for Susanna's ball, he thought. He would call the picture 'The Blue Dress' and everyone would see for themselves what a beautiful wife he had. Then sleep claimed him and he did not wake until late in the afternoon, when he looked for her, fearful lest she had gone.

'I am here,' she said quietly, touching his hand.

'Ah!' He turned his head, smiling. 'Would you like to live in St. John's Wood after we are married?' he asked.

'Not particularly.' She met his lightness with lightness, refusing to take him seriously.

'Or Kensington: in the best part of it—in Palace Gardens, for instance?'

'Not really.'

'Not even near Lord Leighton?'

'No thank you.'

'Irritating woman. You would not object then to Putney and a rather stuffy house and garden, where I could build my studio? Nothing very grand, I'm afraid.'

'But then I'm not very grand,' she said.

'And that is why I love you.' He broke off. 'I can see Sister's strange cap floating down the room like a sail before the wind. She is coming to turn you out. Kiss me, my darling, before you go.'

'Oh, Will!' She hesitated, scarcely able to believe that he was serious after all.

'If you do not kiss me,' he threatened her, 'I shall become so excited that you will never be allowed into the hospital again.'

She stooped to kiss him and as he held her with his uninjured arm he murmured, 'We'll be married just as soon as I can stagger as far as the Embassy, and afterwards I'll take you to that house in Putney and we'll

163

replan it together. But there are some things you must never throw away.'

She released herself gently and stood there smiling down at him. 'What things?'

'Oh, ostrich eggs and peacock feathers and things like that.' He saw her look of alarm. 'I'm not light-headed, my love. They are part of the past, which was also the future that Aunt Clara built for me.'

And then Sister reached his bed and she had to go.

16

While Dinah visited the hospital Susanna, after putting
her head round the door every day to assure herself that
her uncle was still alive, set out on a tour of Paris. It
seemed that Mr. Royde thought she should see something more of that queen of cities than the interior of a
hospital coupled with their salon. He produced a
charming young man by the name of Henry Beresford,
and his equally charming sister, Amy. Henry was employed at the Embassy and the two young people were
delighted to befriend Susanna, taking her for drives in
the Bois de Boulogne, visiting the Louvre, and showing
her the great space being dug for the foundations of
a gigantic steel tower that Mr. Eiffel had designed, to
be built in time for the Exhibition of 1889. They escor-
ted her to the opera and to the theatre, and one day
Henry drove her alone to Fontainebleau, his sister following in a carriage with other friends.

'Mr. Royde appeared to think that you should see
all the things that tourists usually see,' Henry Beresford said as they drew ahead of his sister's carriage.

'I apologise for Mr. Royde,' Susanna said demurely.
'I am afraid it has been a boring occupation for you and
your sister. You both must know it all so well.'

'Nothing, not even the Louvre on a wet day, could be
boring with such a companion,' he replied gallantly.

'They teach you very well at the Embassy, Mr.
Beresford.' Such a compliment from Captain Sloane a
few months ago would have embarrassed and delighted

her, but now she could receive it with composure and a smile.

'It is a hard school, Miss Farebrother.' He sighed. 'One cannot afford the luxury of a wife.'

'Then you must look out for some nice rich girl who will further your career,' she said robustly.

'But rich girls are seldom nice, Miss Farebrother.' He sounded plaintive.

'It is no use looking at me, Mr. Beresford. I am as poor as a church mouse.'

'Church mice are so much more fascinating than any other kind.'

'But they won't butter your bread,' she said, and laughed, and he laughed with her.

The following day Susanna was walking in the Bois de Boulogne with the two young Beresfords when they saw Mr. Royde a little way in front of them, with a family of French people. A little girl had hold of his hand and was looking up into his face, chattering happily, while a lady, who was evidently her mother, was on his other arm, and two boys walked beside them. It looked a happy family party, and in the midst of it Mr. Royde strode along with the customary severity in his face softened a little as he listened to the child. Then suddenly he looked up and saw the three young people in front of him and stopped, raising his hat.

'Miss Farebrother—Mr. Beresford, Miss Amy,' he said with a touch of stiffness. 'I did not expect to see you here. Allow me to introduce Madame Maurel, Master Jean and Master Paul Maurel, and Mademoiselle Charlotte Maurel.'

The Frenchwoman smiled, bowed and said she was enchanted, but the child seemed to think some explanation was necessary for their presence there with Mr. Royde. 'I am always so happy when my Uncle Edward comes to Paris,' she told Susanna solemnly without any

166

of the English child's shyness. 'He is so kind. He gives me everything I want.'

'Hush, Charlotte, be quiet!' Her mother laughed. 'Your uncle's friends will think you a very greedy little girl.'

'But there is something we intend to purchase this afternoon, I believe,' Royde said smilingly. 'A doll, is it not, Charlotte? A *bébé*?' And then to Susanna with grave courtesy, 'You are dining at the Embassy tonight I think. No doubt we shall meet again there.' And once more lifting his hat he went off with his family.

Susanna watched him go with astonishment and concern. The Frenchwoman, though quietly dressed, had not been of the class she thought he would have chosen for his friends, and as they walked on, instinctively taking another direction, she tried to put this feeling into words.

'Mr. Royde told me he would be visiting a lady in Paris,' she said slowly. 'But I had no idea she would be—' She broke off, uncertain of how to proceed and then went on hastily, 'But then I really know so very little about Mr. Royde, though we are neighbours.'

'I believe there was a story circulating about Mr. Royde and an opera singer at one time,' Mr. Beresford said, glancing at his sister.

'Yes,' Amy said. 'I don't know the truth of it of course, but I think it was generally understood that he had a—friend—in the Paris opera some years ago.'

Susanna frowned, remembering stories she had heard in a guarded way about gentlemen—her father among them—who had mistresses in Paris. 'But—that lady looked too respectable to be an opera singer,' she said.

Amy laughed. 'But my dear Miss Farebrother, even opera singers can be very respectable people!'

'Yes, I suppose they can.' But the child's claim of Royde as her uncle still shocked and chagrined her, be-

167

cause she was beginning to realise that what she had said was true: she knew nothing at all about Edward Royde.

She wondered if he would mention the little family to her that night at the private dinner-party at the Embassy, but he did not take her in to dinner and he did not come near her until it was time to go, when he offered himself as her escort back to the hotel. But if she hoped that he might have something to say about his friends in the dark privacy of the carriage, she was disappointed. He told her somewhat abruptly that he had heard from his sister and that she and the Admiral planned to be married in ten days' time. 'But I expect you will have heard from your father to the same effect?' he added.

'I have not heard from him at all.' She tried loyally to make excuses for him. 'Like Captain Ashworth, he hates writing letters.' And then as he tried not to be angry with the man who was marrying his sister she went on: 'Was there any message for me?'

'Yes.' He stared out at the dark streets. 'They want you to go home.'

'Home?' She tried to imagine Waveney with Lady Sare there with her father and failed. Although she had joked and laughed with Dinah about her father marrying again, and had selected improbable ladies for him and even their dearly loved Dorothea, she had never believed that he would marry for a second time. Was she not there now, grown up and ready to act as his hostess?

She had looked forward so intensely to his homecoming but he had not been in Waveney twenty-four hours before he was engaged to Cecily Sare. It was as if a beloved toy had broken in her hand, and she had been glad of the excuse to escape for a time to Paris. She knew that she was being unreasonable: had she not been ready only a few hours before her father's arrival home to greet him with the news of her own

168

engagement to Captain Sloane—knowing now that her feeling for Frank had been nothing more than a passing infatuation? And now that Dinah no longer needed her she knew that she had to face the new situation at home and stop running away.

'My father is very fortunate,' she said. 'He was born with a charm that captivates people and he accepts their love as carelessly as he accepts poor old Bruce's devotion—as his right. I wonder if your sister understands this?'

'I think she does. You must remember that for her too it will be a second marriage. Neither of them will make the demands on each other that they might have made before. They will accept faults as well as recognise the sterling qualities in each other with what I believe to be a very genuine and deep affection.'

'I am glad of that.' She hesitated. 'So they want me to go home?'

'You must be there for the wedding,' he reminded her. He smiled at her encouragingly, but in the light from a street lamp his face looked rather strained as if he had not been enjoying his own stay in Paris very much.

'Oh, of course. Will you be there?'

'Naturally. I have to give my sister away.' He went on, 'I understand that the Countess has offered to have you to stay with her in London while your father is on his honeymoon.'

'Oh no!' She was dismayed. 'Not Aunt Margaret!'

'It will be an experience for you, Susanna, even if you do not enjoy it very much.' Her Christian name slipped out almost unconsciously. 'My sister says—' and here his mouth twisted a little—'that is to say the Countess told her that if you behave yourself she might present you at the first drawing-room next year—either in April or May, whenever Her Majesty chooses to hold one.'

'How charmingly put. One can always count on Great-Aunt Margaret for saying things that will put one in good humour for a start. But I thought Lady Sare was going to present me?'

'The Countess appeared to be offended at the thought that your own relatives were not able to do it for you. I think she plans to give you a few parties and balls, though it is at the end of the season.' He glanced at the grave young face beside him in the gloom of the cab. 'I hope the prospect does not alarm you too much?'

'Not at all.' She lifted her shoulders in a shrug. 'I have never been afraid of Great-Aunt Margaret, and I daresay she means well, though she is a conceited, purse-proud, rude old woman. I will try not to quarrel with her, though, for Papa's sake.' She dismissed her own future plans quickly. 'I do not like the thought of leaving Aunt Dinah alone here. I suppose she is not coming with me?'

'No. And I do not think you need worry about her. The time is soon coming when she will find herself needed elsewhere.'

'You mean—Uncle Will?' She thought of her aunt's face when she had looked down at him that first day in the hospital, for the first time forgetting to keep a tight rein on her emotions.

'I think they will be married as soon as he is well enough to travel.'

'I am so glad for them both.' But Waveney without her aunt and with Lady Sare in command daunted her a little. She knew the time would come when she would learn to love her stepmother dearly, but everything was happening too quickly. She was being thrust now into the tail-end of a London season with an austere relative she did not like and in a way she did not want.

The cab stopped outside her hotel and as he helped her to alight and saw her to the doors of the hotel he said, almost as if he read her thoughts, 'You'll find plenty of young men in London ready to lay their hearts at your feet.'

'Thank you. I wonder if you are right?' Was he being cynical or did he mean it? Either way it was hurtful, because it was so obvious that he did not intend to be there. 'But of course you are right. You always are right—as I am always wrong.'

The note of sarcasm in the young voice cut him to the quick. 'Not wrong,' he protested. 'Only young.'

At that she whipped round on him with all her old fire. 'There you go again!' she cried. 'How often am I to tell you that I am no longer a child?'

'Excellent! Here is the old Susanna back again. I was beginning to be afraid that I had lost her!' He laughed and held out his hand. 'Good night, Miss Farebrother! I stand rebuked.'

She laughed too, suddenly, charmingly, and said, with a quiet dignity that surprised and touched him, 'No doubt Aunt Margaret meant it kindly. She thought she would be ridding my family of an embarrassing responsibility at this time. I will do my best to be properly grateful.' She put her hand into his. 'We shall meet at the wedding then, Mr. Royde, so I will only say *au revoir*.' After she had left him he was conscious of a feeling of anger and guilt because he had seen so little of her during her stay in Paris. He did not trust the old Countess, he had been extremely uneasy ever since he had received his sister's letter, feeling certain that it had not been pure altruism that had prompted the old lady's offer, and he was surprised by the depth of his own concern for Susanna.

She left for England early on the following morning with Jessie, they travelled with a family party from the

Embassy and he did not see her again until the wedding a fortnight later.

Susanna arrived home to find Waveney already under the spell of its future mistress. Mrs. Beswick in particular was loud in her praise of the future Lady Farebrother. She told Perryman that they could be sure of one thing—her ladyship would never hobnob. If she noticed a housemaid with chilblains Mrs. Beswick was ready to take her oath that she would send the girl to the housekeeper, and perhaps enquire after the hands on some future occasion when she was discussing the day's menus with her. As a true lady should. 'If there's one thing I cannot abide,' Mrs. Beswick said, 'it's a lady what's too familiar with her servants.' An added satisfaction was the thought that Lady Sare was leaving her own housekeeper behind her at Royde to look after that large house and her brother there.

Susanna had not been forgotten, and when she arrived home she found a dozen or so dresses waiting for her approval, one apple-blossom pink selected for the wedding, and all made with exquisite taste and detail by Lady Sare's dressmaker in London.

'She made your coming-out dress so well that I had no fear that she would not make others for you equally satisfactorily.' Her future mamma smiled at her affectionately. 'I could not think of sending you to stay with the Countess without a proper wardrobe. I hope you will like them—there was not a great deal of time to get them made—but if there is anything you would like altered we can have it done later on.'

Being fond of pretty things, Susanna tried them on and had no fault to find with any of them. Day dresses, walking dresses, summer dresses in muslin and fine silk, and exquisite evening dresses, they were all lovely and she said so, embracing Lady Sare with real affection.

'It is an apology on my part,' Cecily Sare said smiling.

172

'I owe you more than a few dresses, because I have taken your father away so soon after his home-coming. But it will only be for a month, my dear. We plan to see your Uncle Will in Paris—if he is not married and in Putney by then—on our way to Switzerland, where we shall make a short tour before coming home to you and Waveney.' She studied Susanna anxiously. 'Do you think you will be able to bear with the Countess for a month?'

'I will do my best. Do not look so worried. I am well able to stand my ground with Great-Aunt Margaret. I have never been afraid of her in my life. I am so glad that Papa chose you out of all the ladies he might have chosen if Mrs. Somerton had had her way. Mrs. Taverner, for instance—or Miss Dudley.'

'Oh no! Not Mrs. Taverner! Oh, poor dear John! And Iris Dudley is the biggest snob on earth.' Cecily's eyes met Susanna's and they both laughed.

'You have saved him from a fate worse than death,' Susanna said, and linking her arm in Cecily's she took her down to the rose garden to discuss Lady Sare's plans for it the following year.

As they strolled in the sunshine of that lovely day Cecily Sare said that she was afraid that her brother would miss her very much, though he had never been one to show his feelings.

'I wish he would marry again,' she said. 'But he may have told you that he was visiting Paris because it was the anniversary of his wife's death?'

'No, he said nothing.' Susanna tried not to show the shock of surprise she felt. 'I did not know he was married.'

'Well, I daresay you did not. He never speaks of his wife and neither do I. She was an opera singer and he insisted on marrying her. He was deeply in love and he would listen to none of us—he was very young at the

173

time. But they had only three months together before she died, and for a time I feared he would never get over it. Every year on the anniversary of her death though, he makes sure that he is in Paris to be with her mother, although I think—and hope—this may be the last time. Her eldest son, married and settled in America, has asked her to join him and his family and to make her home with them, and she is leaving for New York next week. I shall be very relieved for my brother's sake if she stays there and does not come back. Although she has always declared that her affection for Odile's husband makes her glad to have him with her at these times I have a feeling that her business sense is engaged in it too. She knows that Edward is a rich man, and after all you cannot cure a wound by keeping it open. When my husband was killed I determined I would not be like the Queen, dwelling on anniversaries, and that directly I was free to do so I would shed my widow's weeds.'

'I think I saw your brother with some of his wife's relations in Paris,' Susanna said hesitatingly, hating herself for probing and yet longing to know more.

'Oh yes. He has been goodness itself to Odile's family: he has seen that her younger sisters have had dowries when they married, and that her brothers have been able to start in any trade or business they might fancy. It is entirely due to him that the eldest boy had the offer of this excellent post in America.' And then spying Grumitt in the distance she went off to discuss with him her plans for the future planting of the rose garden, being careful, however, to defer to him in everything as, Mrs. Beswick would have said, a true lady should.

The wedding took place in Royde village church with many tenants from both estates present, and as many friends and relations from both families who could tear themselves away from London. The Bishop took the

174

service, and wagons with benches in them brought villagers and estate workers from Waveney, and those who could not get into the church lined the path from the porch to the gate. The wedding breakfast was held in the house and afterwards the Admiral and his bride visited the big marquee in the park where the tenants were dining to the music of the Jerningham Town Band.

After her father and the new Lady Farebrother had left for Paris, Susanna moved about among the Waveney people in the park, shaking hands with them, greeting the families and thanking them for their good wishes for her father. And all the time she was conscious of Edward Royde supplying moral support in the background, because sports had been arranged to round off the day, and although he might be taken off to watch the scores on the shooting range and in the bowling alley, or to help the umpire to decide on some knotty point of play in the cricket match in the evening, she felt that he was never far from her and it brought a little comfort to the bleakness of that day. The Ashworths had gone, Dinah was in Paris, and she was alone with the old Countess and she rebelled against a code of conduct that made it impossible for her to remain at Waveney alone without a chaperon.

The next morning she left with the Countess on an early train, taking Jessie with her in great awe of the somewhat contemptuous Miss Tillot. The Countess was a tiresome woman asking innumerable questions that Susanna found slightly impertinent. What was the Admiral's income, now he had retired, and how much, at a rough guess, did it cost him to keep up Waveney, and what was the amount of fortune that he could expect Lady Sare to bring into the family? People said she had as much as ten thousand a year, but was it only hers for life, or had the capital sum it represented come to the Admiral on his marriage?

175

Fortunately Susanna was quite unable to enlighten her on any of these points. She told her that she never discussed money matters with her father.

'Then you should. No girl should be kept in ignorance of the fortune she is to expect from her parents.'

'Oh that is a simple matter for me then, because I do not expect anything at all,' Susanna said, laughing.

'But you will inherit Waveney, child.'

Susanna said with deplorable levity that that would be no benefit to her whatever. 'If it is still free of debt by the time Papa goes,' she said cheerfully, 'there may be another family by that time to share it with me.'

The Countess told her sharply not to be indelicate. 'I presume your father gives you pin money?' she added.

'And a dress allowance,' agreed Susanna good-humouredly. 'No definite sum has been fixed as yet though, and whatever it may be I daresay I shall manage very well on it. I have not been brought up to be extravagant,' she added with a smile that annoyed her great-aunt more than ever.

'No,' she agreed acidly. 'Miss Woodcock had deplorable ideas about money. She scrimped and pinched as if your father was a pauper. And now she is to marry Will—the black sheep of the family. Well, I wish her joy of him.'

'So do I,' said Susanna softly. 'They are both such dears, and I love them so much.'

The Countess said she would like her smelling-salts.

17

It was about a fortnight later that Mr. Royde heard from Mrs. Somerton that Susanna was back at Waveney.

'I knew it would not work,' she told him, meeting him in the High Street one morning. 'That visit of hers to the Countess. Dear Susanna has never learned manners or tact—well, there has been nobody at Waveney to teach her, has there?—and I was certain that the Countess could not approve of her behaviour.'

'Her behaviour?' Mr. Royde frowned.

'Yes. I am very much afraid, Mr. Royde, that Susanna has been sent home in disgrace. And that is not the only thing. I had occasion to write to her to remonstrate with her about something she has done in the last few days since she has been at home and I had a most impertinent letter from her this morning. I shall leave her severely alone for at least a week. I do not feel able to trust myself to speak to her at present.'

While Mr. Royde felt that Susanna might not find this hard to bear he went back to Royde Park in a thoughtful mood and after trying to imagine what the total sum of Susanna's crimes might be, he rode over to Waveney during the afternoon and asked Perryman if Miss Susanna was at home.

'She said she was going to see Grumitt about the carnations, sir. She wants to have 'em on the dining-table end of next week when the H'Admiral and 'er ladyship comes 'ome.'

'I will go and find her.'

'The shortest way to the 'ot-'ouses, sir, is through the morning-room.' He conducted Mr. Royde through the morning-room where he was slightly surprised to find Miss Trot sitting at the round table there stripping lavender for lavender bags. He thought Susanna had finished with governesses long ago. The room smelt of lavender and he left Miss Trot to her task and following the direction pointed out to him by the butler, eventually found himself in the first of the walled fruit gardens, with its crinkle-crankle wall on one side and a row of hot-houses and cold frames on the other. Susanna was just coming out of the far house as he arrived and leaving Grumitt with a smiling word of thanks, and with Bruce lumbering along behind her, she came to meet him, her face bright with pleasure. She did not look at all like a girl who had come home under a cloud from her grand relation's house, nor did she look as if she would write impertinent letters to the Bishop's wife.

'I hear,' he said, as they strolled back towards the house together, 'you have been sent back from London in disgrace?'

She shot a laughing glance at him. 'Who told you that? No, I can guess. You have seen Mrs. Somerton?'

'I have. What on earth happened, Susanna?'

She sighed. 'It was that awful old man,' she said. 'He was a great friend of Aunt Margaret's, and I'd seen him watching me at all the balls I went to, and once he danced with me and it was—horrid. He almost licked his lips over me, as if I were a sugar cake. If you know what I mean.'

'Yes,' he said quietly. 'I think I know what you mean.'

'And then one morning he came to call on Aunt Margaret—at least that was what he said—and I was alone in the small drawing-room when he arrived, and he started trying to continue from where he left off in the dance, and he began to fondle me and kiss me—and I smacked his face.'

'You *what*!' Laughter seized Edward Royde helplessly.

'It wasn't a laughing matter,' Susanna said severely.

'I'm sorry.' He controlled himself with a gasp. 'And what happened then?'

'Why, he left the house in a fury—for which I was thankful, and then Aunt Margaret came in and asked why he had gone and I told her. I said, "That horrible, lecherous old friend of yours started making love to me and so I smacked his face." And *she* was furious. She said, "Do you realise, you stupid girl, that he is a Marquis? And that he is looking for a pretty young girl for a wife? Why do you think I had you here to stay?" And I said that if he had been the King of England and started tricks like that with me he would have received the same treatment, and I was very sorry if she had asked me to London simply to satisfy the unpleasant tastes of her friends. And then she said that evidently I did not know how to behave, and that no doubt I would be happier at Waveney in the company of servants during my father's absence, and I said she was perfectly correct, and I rang for Jessie and she packed and I sent one of the footmen—Aunt Margaret had six —for a cab, and we came home. I was rather short of money and by the time I had paid the cabby and kept sixpence for a tip for the porter, and sent a sixpenny telegram to Honeysett to meet the train at Jerningham I could only afford third-class tickets for Jessie and me. But we travelled down in a carriage full of people going to the Jerningham Races and it was great fun.'

'Susanna, will you ever learn propriety?'

'Never.' Her face broke into laughter again and he knew that it was partly her total disregard for the shib-

179

boleths of others that he found so delightful. He had missed her unbearably since she had been away, and in fact there had been a day when he had turned his back on Royde and gone to London for a few days and had tried to pluck up courage to call on her great-aunt there, and then had changed his mind thinking that there would be plenty of young men like Henry Beresford in Paris, to keep her amused. He said, trying to be severe and not succeeding very well because the warm sympathy he felt for her insisted on creeping into his voice:

'What was the cause of the—impertinent letter—that you sent to Mrs. Somerton?'

'Did she tell you about that?' She looked surprised and then she said thoughtfully, 'I suppose it *was* impertinent because she is so much older than I am and I ought to have gone to see her—or the Bishop. He would have understood, bless him. He is the most understanding person in the world—except perhaps, you!'

She looked at him doubtfully and he said smiling, 'Thank you. I hope you will continue to think so. Tell me about it.'

'Well you see, it was poor old Trot.'

'I noticed your governess was back again. I thought you had finished with them, Susanna!'

'So I have. But you see Mrs. Somerton found this post for her with the horrible Pontypools all in a hurry just before Papa came home, and Aunt Dinah packed her off full of gratitude and indigestion, because poor Trot always gets indigestion when she is excited. Well, we didn't hear from her but there was so much to do with Uncle Will and Papa and my ball and everything that I'm afraid we forgot about her. And then, when I got home from London last week, I found a letter from her waiting for me.' She paused, waiting for Bruce to catch up with them: he was too old to hurry on a warm summer day.

'She didn't complain,' Susanna went on then. 'Trot is a gift to the bullies of this world because she never does complain. She said she was sorry she had not been able to write to me before, and that she had thought about me so much on the day of my ball, and she had managed to find a newspaper that one of the house-maids was using to light the fires, and it had an account of the ball in it and that I had looked—oh well, dear old Trot was always much too complimentary where I was concerned. I could never look plain or badly dressed to her.'

Edward Royde felt a sudden liking for Miss Trot: she was evidently a nice woman, with good taste. 'What else did she say?' he asked.

'It was what she didn't say,' Susanna said, her brows creased in a frown. 'I could not think why she did not see any newspapers. She saw ours the same day that they came: we used to read them together, Trot and Aunt Di and I. And then though she said it was a beau-tiful house and richly furnished she said nothing of her employers or the girl she was teaching. So, as Wentley Parva was only ten miles away, I got Honeysett to take me over there and I arrived at midday. The footman who opened the door said that Miss Trot was having her luncheon in the schoolroom, so I said I would wait for her to finish and he said that didn't matter, as she was alone there and I could step up if I wished. So I step-ped up, and poor darling Trot was sitting there trying to eat a plate of greasy mutton, with an unspeakable watery rice pudding afterwards, and when she saw me she jumped up and ran into my arms. "Susanna!" she cried. "Oh, my darling!" I could feel her shaking and she was hard put to it not to burst out crying, so I said I'd come to see her to find out if she was happy. She said oh yes, quite happy, but I knew she wasn't telling the truth and I asked her if the family was out and was that why she was having her meal alone up there, and she said no, the family always had their meals without her. "They prefer it, dear," she said. "And so do I." When I'd met the people downstairs I did not wonder. But first I asked if I could see her room and she was most unwilling for me to see it, and then as I insisted, she took me upstairs. It was just a garret, with bare boards and a strip of threadbare carpet by her bed—her mattress felt as if it were stuffed with turnips. The wall by her bed was covered in mildew where the damp came in, there were ragged curtains at the window, and in fact it was a room into which Mrs. Beswick would not have dreamed of putting a scullery-maid. I asked what Mrs. Pontypool was like and she tried to make excuses for her. She was sure she meant well, only she did not think she was very experienced in managing servants—she did not think the Pontypools had had money very long, and Mrs. P. treated her rather as if she were a servant. "Not that she means to, dear," she added quickly. "It's just that she doesn't know!" I asked her about her pupil but I could get nothing out of her, and suddenly the abominable child appeared at the door and stalked into the room. "Well, Pig's trotter?" she said. "Are you showing your friend your sty? Mamma is very angry with you, so you had better send your friend away and come downstairs at once." I was so angry that I could scarcely trust myself to speak. Then I said, "Kindly tell your mother that we will come downstairs when we are ready." And I took her by the shoulders and pushed her out of the room and locked the door on her. "Now, Trot," I said, "we'll pack." She tried to protest, but I took no notice. I dragged her portmanteau into the middle of the room and started to empty her clothes into it pell-mell. "Jessie shall iron them for you when we get home," I said. "Home," she said, and then she did cry a little. So I gave her a hug and told her to put

182

her hat on and help me and it was done in no time, and when I came down with her into the hall there was Mr. Pontypool waiting for us with his lady. They were exactly as I had imagined them to be from seeing their horrid child. Mrs. Pontypool was another Mrs. Taverner—only not nearly so nice—and he looked like a pub-keeper from Liverpool. Only I'm not sure what a pub-keeper from Liverpool looks like and I daresay he would be much nicer. He asked me what I thought I was doing, and when I said I was taking Miss Trot home with me he said I'd no right to do that and that she had not worked out her wages. So I drew myself up and I said very icily indeed, "If Miss Trot owes you money out of her—salary—Mr. Pontypool, I have no doubt that my father, Admiral Sir John Farebrother of Waveney, will be delighted to repay you. You will be hearing from his lawyer, Mr. Copthorne, in due course. And in the meantime I will be obliged if you will send one of your footmen to help my coachman downstairs with Miss Trot's portmanteau." I think the mention of Mr. Copthorne did it—or maybe it was Papa's title: I had never met people like that before so that I do not quite know what they consider to be most important. But two footmen were dispatched for the portmanteau right away and Honeysett was not allowed into the house. I took Trot down to the Crown Hotel in the village and the landlady there had a nice lunch sent up to us in a private room. And after that we came home,' she added simply.

He listened to her with indignation and respect, because she had acted with speed and resourcefulness, and because once having made up her mind, nothing would deter her. As it had always been with her. 'And where does Mrs. Somerton come into this?' he asked.

'Oh!' She looked at him and blushed, and then looked away again. They had reached the terrace and she

183

leaned her arms on the stone balustrade, looking out over the countless nodding heads of the marguerites in the park to the golden countryside beyond, while Bruce settled himself beside her in the shade of a stone Juno. 'Mrs. Pontypool met Mrs. Somerton that afternoon at a charity garden-party in the neighbourhood and I don't quite know how she explained it all, but I had a letter from Mrs. Somerton accusing me of "high-handed action" and that I had no right to take poor old Miss Trot from a place where she could live happily for years. And what did I propose to do with her now? I was so angry that I did not choose my words in my reply. I said that if she had imagined Miss Trot could have lived happily for years with the Pontypools perhaps she would like to go and inspect the room she had been given to sleep in, and that in any case I considered my old governess's welfare to be my business and not hers. I'm afraid I was very rude. But then I have often longed to be rude to Mrs. Somerton.'

It was a feeling that Mr. Royde appreciated. 'And what *are* you going to do with Miss Trot?' he asked.

'Oh, there we have had a tremendous stroke of luck.' She was radiant. 'She had a letter this morning from Miss Bentley from the Palace, in which she said—most tactfully—that she had heard that she had not been happy in her new post, and she was glad for her own sake as it meant that she was now free to ask her if she would join her in the little school she was starting in Jerningham in the New Year. She wanted a lady to superintend the little ones, and the children's health and well-being, and she was sure that Miss Trot was the very person for it. Naturally Trot wrote off at once to accept her offer, and now I feel that her future is really assured. I don't quite know what your sister will say about having her here when she comes home, but it will only be until Christmas, and I am sure we can find her odd jobs at Waveney to make her feel that she is needed here.' And then as he did not reply she turned, still leaning against the parapet, her eyes searching his face anxiously. 'Do you think I was high-handed?' she asked. 'Do you think that I should not have interfered?'

'I suppose Mrs. Somerton might argue that had you gone about it in a different way you might have improved Miss Trot's position with those people.'

She shook her head. 'Not with them. You had only to *see* Mr. Pontypool!'

'Then as things have turned out you were right to act as you did. Sometimes when we act on impulse it saves a situation—sometimes the reverse. And she has given you years of affection—if not a great deal of learning perhaps.'

'Oh no. It was Miss Bentley who taught me French and Latin and mathematics, all far beyond dear old Trot. But I don't think you can learn about people in the schoolroom, Mr. Royde. You know nothing about them by the time you have left lesson books behind you. To me every man was a potential hero.' She laughed up at him.

'Except me,' he said gravely, but his eyes were twinkling again.

'Oh, I detested you!' she replied. 'From the day when I was fifteen and you found me stuck in an old pear tree in the far orchard. Do you remember?'

'I remember it very well.'

'You said, "Miss Farebrother, climbing trees in a young lady may be considered to be hoydenish, at the least, but for anybody to climb a pear tree of that age, with brittle branches that might snap off at any moment, is also foolhardy and dangerous. I will help you down if you promise not to do it again."'

'What a prig you must have thought me!' he said. 'But I did help you down, and when I wanted you to

185

promise not to climb any more trees you made a saucy little curtsey and said, "I believe the bargain was for pear trees only, Mr. Royde!" I could have spanked you.'

'I liked climbing trees,' she said frankly. 'I could escape from life into a green world of my own. I was very much alone at Waveney—and the Somerton girls were so prim. That was why, I suppose, I behaved so badly when I was young. Aunt Dinah did her best to make up for Papa, but she could not quite manage it and she knew it. You see when he came home on leave he treated me much as he treated old Bruce here: he acknowledged my affection with a pat on the head and then forgot about me. In the winter he could think of nothing but hunting, and in the summer there was fishing—and the estate. Always the estate. It was so heavily mortgaged that it was naturally more important in his eyes than a mere daughter.'

'Life is full of surprises,' he said quietly. 'You think your own flesh and blood will understand you, but they don't. You think your dearest friend will never betray you—and he does. You think your heart is broken—and it isn't.' He leaned his elbows on the balustrade beside her, looking across as she had done at the spreading countryside. 'I thought,' he said then deliberately, 'that I would never fall in love again—but I have.' He gave a wry little smile. 'I give you full permission to laugh at me, Susanna!'

'But why should I do that?' A great coldness descended upon her and the light in her eyes was suddenly extinguished. Somebody else—some woman in Paris perhaps—had captured him, would be his to love and cherish, would be happy to love and obey him. And she would be more alone than she had ever been before. It was only in that moment that she knew what he had meant to her over the years, though she had guessed it

186

on the night of the ball when he had brusquely told her to put up her head and hold her shoulders back. 'What is she like?' she asked.

'She is much younger than I am, and I'm afraid she will feel that to be a barrier between us. She knows her own mind and she does not hesitate to speak it—giving offence sometimes to her elders and betters. No, I will not say betters, because in my mind she has none. If she should marry me we would quarrel I daresay from time to time, because we know each other well enough to be able to quarrel, and although I would swear that I would not let her have her own way I'm afraid she would be able to twist me round her little finger and get it in the end. But I think, because I know her so well. she would sometimes let me have my way too.'

'Have you—asked her yet?' There was a tremor in Susanna's voice.

'No, I'm rather afraid to, because when older men make love to her she has a habit of smacking their faces.'

He saw her head come up and her eyes meet his, and then her hand came up too and he caught it just in time before it could administer what would have been a merited if somewhat stinging rebuke.

'You wretch!' she cried. 'You utter wretch! Letting me think that it was somebody else—that I—had lost you for ever!'

'Does that mean that—old as I am—you will marry me, Susanna?'

'Just you try to marry somebody else. I'll make such a scene that you will never do it again!' Susanna collapsed in laughter and clasped her arms round him, laying her head on his heart.

'Those windows,' he said, glancing at the south front of Waveney, 'have a thousand eyes and I am not used to being embraced in public. I feel this is the time when

187

a shrubbery has its uses.' He caught her round the waist and took her off briskly to where tall masses of rhododendrons and laurels hid a wilderness of small mossy paths. It was not quite as secluded as he had imagined however. Grumitt was leading the way through the far end of it to the park where there was a pile of well-matured leaf-mould, followed by an under-gardener with a wheelbarrow, when he happened to glance down one of the mossy paths and seeing the two people there oblivious of anyone except each other, he immediately turned about, saying that he had just remembered the gate was locked and he had not got the key with him.

Being Grumitt he said no more, but to himself he said a great deal. 'Miss Susanna and Mr. Royde. H'm. He'll keep her in order maybe, and she'll teach him to laugh. It ought to work out right between them—in fact it ought to be a very 'appy do.'

It was an opinion shared—with the possible exception of Mrs. Somerton—by all their friends.